DEADLY FRIENDSHIP

Tara Lyons

To
Cassandra

With love,
Tara Lyons
x

First published in 2017 by Bloodhound Books

www.bloodhoundbooks.com

Print ISBN 978-1-912175-41-3

Also by Tara Lyons

Read the first two books in the DI Hamilton series

In the Shadows

No Safe Home

Praise for Tara Lyon's No Safe Home, the second book in the DI Hamilton series.

"No Safe Home in my opinion is the author's best novel to date. This book was full of chills and thrills that shocked and surprised me."

Sarah Hardy – By The Letter Book Reviews

"No Safe Home ticked all the boxes for me. It is fast paced and gritty and definitely a must read I cannot recommend it enough, giving it 5 massive gold stars."

Shell Baker – Chelle's Book Reviews

"It is a very complex story with many red herrings and curve balls. The author expertly created well developed characters and a multi-faceted storyline that grabs the readers from the first page."

Jill Burkinshaw- Books n All

"No Safe Home is a fascinating psychological thriller novel about the lasting impact of domestic violence on a person's life. Despite the grimness of the topic in this novel, it is an easy, enjoyable read. A fast paced excellently written novel."

Caroline Vincent – Bits About Books

"Whilst reading the closing chapters I suddenly realised I was holding my breath. the plot moves at a swift, exciting pace making the book hard to put down."

Emma Welton – Damppebbles Book Blog

“There are times when you read a strong opening of a book, or the first few chapters, then the story falters. In No Safe Home Lyon’s didn’t let up the intensity. Whether it was from the crimes, Hamilton’s home life to the various flashbacks.”

Alexina Golding – Bookstormer

For my dearest friends, your love and support continue to inspire me.

PROLOGUE

It wasn't the first time I had thought about killing someone. But it was the first time I had acted on my instincts.

For a moment, I don't think the concoction of drugs in her vodka and tonic is enough to knock her out. She's dancing barefoot, and the long wisps of grass slide in and out of her toes. Her pink dress swishes around her knees as she slowly spins; her white arms extend out to the descending sun, content in this moment of tranquillity. I watch the last rays of the day glisten across the freckles dotted on her nose and cheeks. Her short, dark hair has been diluted by the frivolous summer heat. I know every strand and mark on her perfect body.

She stumbles and reaches for my arm to steady herself.

'Fuck me, I think I've had one too many,' she says, with a giggle, and knocks a drink over on the table. 'Will you help me to bed? I think I'll sleep it off.'

I wait for her to look at me, but she doesn't. She's too busy thinking of herself to notice the pain engraved on my face. If she just takes one moment for me, if she meets my eyes right now, I'll stop all this. I'll save her.

'Did you hear me?' Her tone's harsher, harder. 'I told you to help me inside. I feel sick.'

Her control over her body falters further, and she tries to lean on me. I step back, allowing her to crumble to the ground, and her head squashes the green blades of grass beneath her. Through the gurgles, I just about make out her muted screams. More demands and instructions aimed at me. Hopelessly thrashing about, she uses the last of her energy.

'What are you doing?' she mumbles.

Her body has totally abandoned her now; she has no control. I'm surprised she managed to get those last words out. With her face in the mud, I kneel down and breathe in her scent. The heat rises in my cheeks. Her perfume always has that effect on me.

Lowering myself, I lay next to her and whisper, 'I was your friend. I was your lover.'

The corner of her mouth twitches. A rattling laugh, deep from the pit of her stomach, rolls from her mouth, and the twitch becomes a smirk.

I jump up, the anger inside burning. Every pore of my skin is on fire. Blinded by the exploding pain in my head, I march around her body. The echo of her laughter mocking me.

Grabbing the kitchen knife from the patio table, I fall to my knees and plunge the sharp tip into her back. A deep groan involuntarily escapes my lips.

Raising my arm, I let the weapon soar high in the air, as the sun melts into its beautiful orange grave. Gripping the handle with both hands, I straddle her arse and strike the knife into her back, over and over again.

The beads of sweat dripping from my forehead mingle with her splashes of blood. They become one, trickling down my face. My racing heart beats with such force, I swear it's preparing to explode right through me, jump from my body in a moment of excitement. I need to calm down and exhaling slowly, I close my eyes and fall forward. Our wet, blood-soaked bodies connect, and I'm content; overwhelmed with pleasure. The woman who betrayed me finally gets what she deserves.

You see, she wasn't who I thought she was. I discovered the hard way that she's a slag. I fell in love with her, harder and faster than ever before – ever at all, if I'm honest. That's why the punishment was fitting to her crime. I would have done anything for her. She was my best friend. My soulmate. She was more than just the woman I loved; we had a deeper connection. Beneath the layer of lust, of hard and fast, animalistic sex, there was devotion, and together, we belonged there. We had shared things with each other – moments from my past I had promised myself I'd never utter to another individual, but she knew. She knew me. She knew everything.

When you trust your friends with your deepest and darkest secrets, it's their duty to keep them, isn't it? But if you discover the foundation of that relationship was built on lies, doesn't it become your duty to end it? Bring a stop to the betrayal, before it consumes you.

Ask yourself, how well do you really know the people you trust?

CHAPTER ONE

Denis Hamilton stood on the wooden pier and gazed out at the calm lake, the mist finally rolling off the waves. The picturesque mountains, framing the scene like an immaculate water painting, now broke free of the thick fog which had kept them captive all weekend. He sucked in the cold air through his nose, filled his lungs, and held it for a few seconds, before releasing it with a deep moan.

It was a far cry from London town, where the air was thick and smoky. Tainted, not only by the vehicles and machinery, but by the death and destruction he witnessed every day. He grunted to himself, thinking how difficult it had always felt to leave work and the bustling city because, after all, he was proud to call London his home. Yet, as he stood watching the boat sails waving in the wind, surrounded by the blues and greens and oranges of Mother Nature, Denis wasn't sure if he ever wanted to leave.

'Come on, love! We don't want to miss the boat,' Philippa called out, from further down the lake.

Denis smiled and gave his mother a small wave. He retraced his steps, pulling his scarf higher around his ears as he briskly walked across the shingle shore.

'Your mum was just telling me some history about Wray Castle,' Elizabeth said, as he reached the jetty leading to the lake. 'I can't believe we've never visited.'

He wrapped his arms around his wife's waist and drew her closer into him. Her emerald green eyes ablaze, the apparent excitement radiated from her.

'You do enjoy a good boat trip, babe,' he said.

'Cut it out, lovebirds.' Philippa laughed, and marched towards the vessel.

Denis and Elizabeth held hands and followed his mother along the dock. As one of the crew members helped the women to step aboard, he cast an eye over the brown, wooden boat. It was small, only one level, but he guessed there were at least forty people sat waiting for their trip. Its name, embossed in gold lettering, read: *Queen of the Lake, Windermere Lake Cruises.*

Despite the early morning breeze, most of the passengers had chosen to brave the weather, sitting at the bow of the boat. Philippa followed suit, claiming the last bench in the middle, directly in front of the cabin. The crew member who'd helped them took his place at the helm, but not before sharing a lingering look with his mother.

'Oh yeah!' Denis elbowed her in the ribs. 'Got yourself a toy boy, have you?'

Philippa's cheeks flushed crimson, and her eyes darted away from his stare. 'And so what if I have? I don't kiss and tell, son.'

He couldn't contain his laughter. Although Philippa was obviously embarrassed by his observation, she remained her usual feisty self. His father had left them both, returning to his home town on Jamaica, when Denis was only fifteen. In the twenty-four years since then, he couldn't remember his mother having many dates, let alone any relationships. While strange to think of his mother in that way, he could appreciate how lonely she must be. Retiring to the tranquil area of Ambleside was a drastic change after more than half a century living in central London.

'Good for you, Mum. As long as you're happy.' Denis winked as the boat revved to life.

Once the second member of the vessel's crew was finished instructing them on safety and tour timings, he began the sight-seeing speech, which he had clearly memorised long ago.

'Did you hear that, Denis?' Elizabeth exclaimed. 'Wray Castle is the mock-gothic building of Cumbria … And Beatrix Potter spent the summer there when she was eighteen.'

He nodded enthusiastically, letting his wife repeat everything the crew member had already informed them of over the microphone. The two of them, childhood sweethearts and married in their early twenties, were always so busy with work, and bringing their work home with them. Here, he felt a deep sense of inner peace.

Philippa broke through the serenity of his thoughts when she extracted a small, metal pole from her handbag. He watched in horror as the rod doubled in size, and she attached her mobile phone to a black clip on one end.

'What the hell –'

'It's selfie time,' Philippa interrupted.

'Mum … you have a selfie-stick?'

'Of course, and a Facebook and Twitter account. Didn't you know? Mary Berry follows me. She must love all the tweets about my little tea shop and the scones we make.'

Denis and Elizabeth laughed together. 'I'm shocked, Mum.'

'Why, because I'm sixty-five? Pah! I'm down with the kids, Denis. You need to step up and join in with the new way of doing things.'

Despite his mother's comment being a playful one, it pinched his heart all the same. His daughter, Maggie, had committed suicide five years ago, at the age of sixteen, due to ongoing cyberbullying. Since the day his world fell apart, he'd always been averse to social media. As painful as it was, he shook the sad memory from the forefront of his mind, intent on enjoying the day with his mother and wife.

'You never know, Mum. I could be incognito online, watching your every move,' he said and summoned a noise which sounded like a laugh.

'Ooh,' Philippa replied, as she fiddled with the positioning of her phone. 'You know who is on Facebook … Anne Thorn. She told me her Billy was in therapy, but wouldn't go into the details. Do you know what that's about?'

Denis's back stiffened and his jaw twitched at the mention of Billy Thorn. 'Not a clue,' he said through gritted teeth.

His mother's attention jumped once again. 'Got it! Right, it's working. You two lovebirds, squeeze in. Let's try and get that sign with the boat's name in the picture too.'

The three of their faces came to life on the iPhone screen. Elizabeth giggled as she pressed her face against his, while Philippa did the same on the other side. Their skin looked pale against his caramel complexion and dark eyes; his mixed-race heritage, the only thing he'd inherited from his father. His black short beard was cut with military precision. His wife, the school headmistress, usually so meticulous with her looks during working hours, had allowed her shoulder-length, auburn hair to hang un-styled, the slight curls blowing freely in the breeze. Denis suddenly realised how much his mother had aged. Though the fringe of her cropped, white hair hid her forehead, he could now clearly see the wrinkles gathering at her eyes and mouth, the skin on her cheeks looser than before. But her eyes still shone brightly, like sapphire crystals beneath a greying face. He looked at himself, sandwiched between the two women in his life, and an invisible punch struck him hard in the gut. It quickly dawned on him there should be three women surrounding him. But he smiled for the photograph regardless, content on making his mother happy.

'Not too far to go now,' Philippa called out, once she was satisfied with the dozen selfies, although Denis was adamant they all looked the same. '*The Queen of the Lake* will continue on its tour, but we'll jump off at the first stop.'

Like mirror images, his mother and wife simultaneously turned their backs on him to enjoy the last leg of their voyage. The boat roared forward, a trail of foam left in its wake, and droplets of water splashed in from the lake, lightly spraying his face. Denis tipped his head back, breathing in the fresh air once again. That rich air, which tickled every nose hair and brought tears to his eyes. They'd only been travelling on the vessel for twenty minutes, but the mist had cleared, giving way to a new day, with bright blue skies and just a few clouds left dancing around the tips of the mountains.

He closed his eyes. The boat began to slow as the crew member announced their arrival at Wray Castle boat house. A shrill scream shattered the calmness, and Denis jumped to attention. His view was blocked. Passengers were on their feet, pointing and yelling, while others covered their faces and tried to shield their children. One of the crew members barged through the crowd, ordering everyone to remain in their seats. Denis ensured both Elizabeth and Philippa were safe, before following the crew member to the very front of the boat.

The vessel danced in the water, the current slowly drawing it closer towards the boat house. Denis held onto the edge and looked out to the Victorian stone building, surrounded by a dense forest and tall oak trees. His attention narrowed on the wooden boat house gate, its ancient and weather-beaten panels a beacon of history and tourism. A length of thick rope travelled down from the metal lock to the water and met a large, white hand, its coarse fibres scorching ligature marks on the wrist.

A man's lifeless body gave in to the resistance of the noose; dangling awkwardly, head and torso bobbing in the water, the rest of his body submerged in the lake. His head hung back, dark hair dipping in and out as he moved with the current. The blood-soaked clothes were useless at concealing his athletic physique. And, despite the colour of death snaking up the man's chiselled jaw line, attacking his lips and cheeks, his unblemished skin revealed a handsome and youthful appearance. There was something stuck in his mouth, but the angle of his head made it difficult to see clearly.

How is a young, muscle man like this, overpowered and abandoned so cruelly? Denis thought with a shudder.

He wanted to look away, but he couldn't tear his gaze from the man's cold eyes, fixated on the same sky he'd been admiring moments before. Or from the man's blood, staining Lake Windermere's beauty.

CHAPTER TWO

After the Cumbria Constabulary and Lake District National Park's Windermere Lake Wardens had been informed of the situation, Denis set about recording as many names of the passengers as possible. He knew he didn't have the authority, or manpower, to stop anyone from leaving the jetty and escaping to the safety of the castle, but he'd swiftly entered professional mode without a second thought. He understood, only too well, the damage an investigation could suffer at the loss of potential witnesses.

'What do you want my bloody name for? Who are you?' a man in his late fifties retorted, after he'd been asked for his details.

'My name is Detective Inspector Denis Hamilton of the London Metropolitan Police, sir.'

'Bit out of your jurisdiction, isn't it?'

'Wrong place, wrong time, I suppose. Or not, depending how you look at things,' he replied with a fake smile; he was no longer on holiday. 'I just thought if you left your details with me, I could pass them onto the constabulary, rather than force your children here to gawk at a dead body for heaven knows how much longer.'

The man nodded his balding head and glanced at the small twins clinging to his burgundy, cord trousers. 'Yes. Yes, you're quite right. But … do you have any identification? I wouldn't want to tell any old stranger my name. I mean, as you said, there is a dead man floating in Lake Windermere.'

'Of course, I completely understand.' DI Hamilton reached inside his coat and retrieved his ID badge.

'Doesn't he ever leave that thing at home?' his mother whispered from behind him.

'Don't be silly, Phil. He's a glass-half-empty kinda guy, always thinks it's needed,' Elizabeth murmured in reply.

Hamilton glanced over his shoulder and raised his eyebrows at the women. In less serious circumstances, their cheeky grins would have enticed a snigger from him. But they knew him well enough to understand banter was not on the cards right now.

After a discussion with the crew members of the *Queen of the Lake*, Hamilton decided it best to evacuate the boat. It was not the view they'd expected, or paid for, but more importantly, he didn't want the crime scene contaminated any further than it had been.

'Please understand, we are not making you stay here against your own free will,' Hamilton said, addressing the crowd once they were all on dry land. 'However, if you would like to speak to the local officers when they arrive, then please feel free. But if I could ask you all to at least follow the pathway and congregate closer to Wray Castle. This now an official crime scene. Put your mobile phones away.'

Some of the passengers tutted at Hamilton's reprimand for taking photos, while others marched off in the opposite direction.

'What should we do, son?' Philippa touched his shoulder to get his attention.

'You and Elizabeth head off, Mum. Maybe you could get a warm drink in the castle, or something?'

'I'm not sure ... shouldn't we stay with you?' his wife argued.

'No. I don't want you freezing your bits off waiting for me. Go on. I'll have a quick chat with the locals when they get here and meet you afterwards,' Hamilton said and gently kissed Elizabeth on her cheek.

As he watched his mother and wife climb the path towards the castle, he was distracted by a beautiful woman ambling towards him. The stranger looked out of place. With the earthy trees and greenery encircling her, she advanced in a short, pinstripe skirt suit and crisp pink shirt. He followed her long, tanned legs and was surprised to see her strolling in a pair of gleaming white

Converse trainers. Her face was sun kissed, the sign of a recent holiday – abroad, not the shores of Ambleside – and the blonde highlights in her light brown hair seemed to glisten as she moved. Abruptly, the woman stopped and checked her phone. She spun in a circle, until her eyes landed on Hamilton.

'I don't suppose you could help me, could you?' she said, with a London accent he knew well.

He gravitated towards her. 'What seems to be the problem?'

'Is this the castle boat house? I'm supposed to be meeting someone here, but I can't seem to find him.'

Hamilton frowned, briefly peered over his shoulder, and wondered if the woman could be looking for their corpse in the lake.

'My boss sent me a text last night and told me to come here,' she continued.

He took a few steps closer and introduced himself, explaining he couldn't permit her to move any closer to the water.

'Why? What's happened?' she questioned.

'Could you tell me your name? Do you live or work around here?' Hamilton countered her questions, wanting to find out more.

'Claire Newcomb. And, no, I don't live here …'

He sensed the woman's hesitation to give him any more information. Despite wanting to probe further, Hamilton remembered he was nowhere near his patch and decided to back off.

'The Cumbria Constabulary officers are on their way, Claire. It might be a good idea to stick around and have a chat with them. I'm sure it's purely coincidental you can't locate your boss, but better safe than sorry.'

She glanced over his shoulder, but Hamilton was confident she couldn't see beyond the building to where the man remained chained to the boat house gate. Claire nodded and returned to her phone.

Crowds of people, a multitude of voices, and equipment being hauled at a quick pace erupted into the quietness of the National

Trust grounds. Hamilton turned around and spotted the Lake Wardens speeding across the lake. The locals were here to take control. He just hoped they wouldn't kick him to the kerb and ignore all his efforts.

* * *

Hamilton stood on the side-lines while a swirl of forensic teams donned shoe covers and protective clothing. A private white tent had been erected, and divers submerged themselves in the lake. It was a rare event to be present at a crime scene for such a long period of time before evidence was collected. He was chomping at the bit to uncover information.

Inspector Ray Bennett of the Cumbria Constabulary was a man in his late fifties, who held no immediate charisma, and the stench of stale coffee oozed from his mouth. Brown caffeine stains coloured the man's greying moustache, and Hamilton subtly held his breathe while Bennett spoke, for fear of vomiting on his new Nike walking trainers.

'It's a good thing you were here, Hamilton, and I appreciate your swift actions,' Bennett said and introduced the two police community support officers who followed his every move.

There was no urgency from the three local coppers, but Hamilton smiled and nodded, refusing to let his frustration get the better of him. If they were in London, he'd already be speaking to the pathologist in charge and demanding clues to propel the case forward. He missed his own murder investigations team.

'Do you think it would be okay if I stuck around?' he asked.

'Aye, I don't see why not,' the older man replied in his deep, Cumbrian accent. 'You've been a great help. My PSCOs can take your statement and any other notes you've gathered.'

The surge of water from beyond the boat house catapulted Hamilton into action. With the body released from the lake, he circled the area, stopping directly outside the forensic tent. A young officer held his palm in Hamilton's face, halting any further progress.

'Don't worry, officer,' Bennett said. 'He's not one of us, but the lad's with me.'

Hamilton slowly turned his head and raised an eyebrow at the local Inspector. *There really is a reek of shit coming from your mouth,* he thought – just one of the insults swimming through his mind. He shrugged, accepted the shoe covers, and remained silent. Entering the tent, he decided to play nice, for just a little while longer at least.

No introductions were made once the men were inside, which didn't bother Hamilton. Yet, something pulled him, a yearning ache to find out more. He couldn't decide if, given his day job, it was purely curiosity, or if there was something more. Could it really just be a coincidence he was on the boat that morning?

The pathologist, a white lady with a light brown, circular birthmark under her left eye, busied herself around the victim, who now lay in the centre of the tent. The camera shutter clicked constantly as the team of forensics worked seamlessly around each other, gathering whatever evidence they could find.

'Is your team collecting evidence from the surrounding forest, namely for any shoe imprints?' Hamilton asked.

'What's the need for that?' Bennett interrupted, before the pathologist had a chance to answer. 'The victim's fully clothed; we can get a sample from his footwear.'

'I find it very unlikely the victim entered the water and tied himself to the gate. Whoever did this would have needed to get in and out of the lake; they would have been dripping with water,' Hamilton replied.

'Ah. Well, yes …'

'It hasn't rained lately, foggy, yes, but surely the near-by vicinity would alert you to any recent footprints. Unless, of course, they travelled to and from the scene by boat.'

'Yes … exactly what I thought too.'

Hamilton crossed his arms, nodding with a frown and sarcastic pout. He didn't care if it was immature; he enjoyed watching the man squirm. *That's what you get for calling me "lad."*

The pathologist cleared her throat. 'My team have it all under control. However, it's this attracting my initial interest,' she said, her American accent a surprise to Hamilton; he suddenly felt less unsettled, since he was no longer the farthest from home.

She reached her gloved hand into the forensic case at the head of the dead body. With what looked like a pair of tweezers, the pathologist extracted a balled-up piece of paper. The three of them squinted, reading the hand-written words over and over again.

Hamilton straightened up and looked back and forth between the pair. 'Who the hell is Donna Moran?'

CHAPTER THREE

I didn't intend on waiting until Warren's body was found, but I'm glad I did. Watching the scene unravel is a thing of beauty. However, there's a copper at the scene. He's different to the others. Oozes confidence and authority, and the way he springs into action highlights his law enforcement training. His presence is unfortunate; going from witness to witness, taking names, and containing the area before it's tainted further. Fucking arsehole.

I couldn't foresee that happening, but I'll need to be more careful in the future. He's nothing like the local policemen, who are stiff and uninterested about the events unfolding before them, if only they took a minute to look around. There's something about this copper, a swagger, and a fire in his eyes. Plus, the London accent wasn't lost on me. He may be a problem.

But the look of sheer panic and fear on the faces of those people running from the boat, as they realise a river of blood flows with the fresh lake water, cheers me. I made that happen. The thrill touches every nerve in my body like an electric shock.

It won't be the last time either, I know that now. I've started my quest to find answers. To discover why they did what they did. I won't rest until I know. No matter the cost.

You see, I've learnt before you can become the very best version of yourself – the hero of your own story – you have to hit rock bottom first. Only then do things become clear. You drag yourself up from the pit of hell, because it's in that moment you understand the person you want to be. The person you were put on this earth to become.

My life's broken apart on more occasions than I want to remember, each time crueller and more heart-breaking than the time before. But in 2015, my world shattered beyond repair. I lost my soulmate and contemplated what was left for me in this wretched existence.

Until six months ago, when my moment of clarity came. I recognised then that I am not weak. I will not be disregarded as someone unworthy to have what everyone else has. I am in control of my destiny, but the people in my life have shaped the decisions I've recently had to make.

They've weaved their lives – their hopes, their fears, and their secrets – into my own.

When I plunged the needle in Warren's neck and then the knife into his back, it came from a place of hate. An emotion that's been there for a long time – since I'd murdered *her* on that delightful summer evening – but one I'd suppressed for many years. Warren awoke that and forced my hand. As the hot volcano of disgust erupted in my stomach, the sharp point of death pierced his flesh. He needed to feel what I felt. He needed to suffer for taking what I had wanted with all my heart.

Yes, I do have a heart, and it's filled with passion.

The blood poured from him and onto my hands. He gasped, but only briefly, before a gurgling noise took over, and the devil came to take his soul. His eyes widened, bulged until I thought they'd pop right out of their sockets and dangle by a blood vessel onto his cheek. I smile at the thought. It would certainly have ruined the perfect image he'd fashioned for himself; desperate for everyone to admire. Not me.

The poison in the syringe had taken effect, and I gripped his shoulder, almost hugging him, while twisting the knife through his flesh, plunging as deep as physically possible. A single stream leaked from the corner of his eye. My hate turned to anger. The man who could have had whatever he wanted, whomever he wanted, had ruined my life. He had called himself my friend, but mocked and teased me at every opportunity. Did he really think crocodile-tears could save him now?

He was helpless. Just as I had felt for most of my life. He couldn't run, or overpower me, or scream for help. My plan had been foolproof. I knew his greed and prying nature would entice him into this trap. To the place where my life had ended two years previously. And, just as the mist rolled away from the lake, I exhaled all the pain and rage I'd clung to.

My only wish, in that moment before Warren's death, was that I uncover the truth. Despite his brief begging and bargaining, I realised, for the first time, he knew nothing. I thought he had been the master, but perhaps I've been wrong all along. He was merely a player in this web of duplicity. However, even the players are accountable, and I will make sure everyone in this game of dishonesty pays the price. The people in my life have shaped the decisions I've made in the past twelve months.

They've weaved their lives – their hopes, their fears, and their secrets – into my own … because they are my friends.

The people who show you support, love, and compassion. But what happens when those very people betray you, ridicule you, and kill you with honesty?

I'll go all the way for my friends, do anything necessary. Wouldn't you?

CHAPTER FOUR

Hamilton's right foot involuntarily tapped the cobble ground as he sat outside his mother's tea room. His eyes were pinned to the area where he'd stood that morning, during what should have been a relaxing, long weekend away. Nothing like a dead body to bring you crashing back to reality. The distance across the water meant he wasn't actually sure if he was looking at the precise location; it was purely guess work.

'Ah, Fraser! You're still in the office,' he said, when the call connected.

'Hey, boss. Can't you take one weekend off?' She laughed. 'We've been working on a brutal rape case this weekend, and all hands-on-deck.'

'How are Rocky and Dixon getting along?' Hamilton asked about the two newest members of the team. The guilt continued to gnaw at him for making use of the bank holiday weekend and escaping to Ambleside; he should have been at the office with them.

'Fitting in really well. You still back tomorrow?'

'Yeah, but driving back on a bank holiday Monday, it'll take about six hours. Minimum.'

Fraser sucked the air through her teeth. 'Don't envy you, boss.'

'No. Look, I was wondering if you could do me a favour … if you find yourself with any spare time?'

'Shoot.'

Hamilton quickly brought his detective sergeant, Kerry Fraser, up to speed about the discovery his tourism boat had made, and everything he'd learnt since. In spite of his wife asking him to leave things to the local constabulary, he couldn't let it go.

'So, why do you want me to look into this Donna Moran?' Fraser asked.

'I had a chat with my mum, and she seems to remember something from a few years ago, about a girl who went missing from Ambleside. I've done a quick Google search, but can't bloody find much. Anyway, it was thought she was only here visiting with friends. I can't understand why there's no newspaper report, or something. How can there be such little information on the web? I thought it was this fantastic tool no-one could do without,' he ended sarcastically.

Fraser sniggered. 'Sometimes, you have to know the right keywords and phrases to search for. Especially with older news articles. Leave it with me, boss. I'll show you how it's done.'

'I've got my laptop with me and have been debating with myself about logging on … having a look through the Missing Persons database,' he said and slightly glanced around the quiet patio area.

'I can only imagine you're telling me, and haven't actually already done it, because you know you are off duty, boss.'

He sighed. 'Yes … not professional. And, in all honestly, I'm not sure who's going to clout me first, my mum or Elizabeth, if I spend another minute on "a flipping case that isn't even on my patch,"' he said in a high-pitched, mocking tone. 'But, maybe, I should listen to them. I am outnumbered.'

'I'll see what I can do this end before you're back in the office on Tuesday.'

'Cheers, Fraser. I appreciate it.'

After Hamilton disconnected the call, he sighed and stood up. The need to spend the last evening with his mother was paramount, but he still couldn't shake the annoyance he felt. The more he thought of the victim rescued from the restraints of the castle's boat house, the more he felt a familiarity towards the man. Hamilton was desperate to know why the victim died, the significance of Donna Moran's name, and if she was a potential victim.

Pleased he'd slipped his business card to the pathologist, he could only hope she'd use it and quench his thirst relating to this case. For now, he pushed it to the back of his mind as best he could. His team were dealing with a scumbag rapist in London, and his family demanded his attention.

* * *

On Tuesday morning, Hamilton dashed from his home at the crack of dawn and beat the morning traffic to the station in Charing Cross. He was overjoyed to find Fraser hunched over her computer keyboard when he entered the incident room. Her long, blonde hair fell around her shoulders and back, while she busied herself with research, as usual.

'Don't you ever go home?' he called out.

'No rest for the wicked, boss,' she said, without taking her eyes off the screen.

Hamilton took a seat next to her. Lifting one foot onto his knee, he reclined slightly in the chair and waited for her to finish.

Fraser clapped her hands and finally turned to face him. She never wore make-up at work, but it suited her, accentuating her youthful, fresh face. There were not many thirty-year-old women who would venture into a male dominated workforce and not feel the need to rely on good, old-fashioned war paint, Hamilton thought.

'Okay, I was here late last night concluding the rape case so I could move onto what you asked first thing this morning,' she said. 'Wait, I assume you saw the news last night?'

He rolled his eyes. 'Of course, I did! London reality TV star murdered on the shores of Lake Windermere, I think the headline was. How do they always get this information so fast?'

'Well, Warren Speed was engaged to a journalist. They announced it about six months ago. They were very much in love and had known each other since …' Fraser stopped rambling when Hamilton closed his eyes and began snoring. 'I take it you don't follow celebrity news?'

'Really, he's a celebrity?'

'You don't watch reality TV then, boss?'

'No, I flaming well don't. It's a load of old crap. You seriously expect me to sit at home watching a programme about people in their homes, eating take-aways, and watching *their* televisions. What the hell is that about?'

'Actually, Warren Speed won Big Brother.'

Hamilton raised his hand to stop Fraser's speech about a group of people who had given up their human rights by choosing to live in a house in Borehamwood with complete strangers.

'Warren Speed can wait for now; he's in the hands of the Cumbria Constabulary. Did you find anything out about the mysterious name that came with him?'

'That I did,' she said and sieved through a few papers on her desk. 'Okay … Donna Moran, who would now be twenty-three, went missing when she was twenty-one, after spending a weekend at the Lake District with her university friends. An only child, her single mother, Joan Moran, reported her missing when her pals returned to London without her. They lived in Maida Vale at the time, and that's the current contact information for the mother on the MisPer database.'

'Right, okay. I want a list of the friends who accompanied her on the getaway, maybe they can shed some more light on this. We'll also need to visit her mother as a matter of urgency. This isn't something she should hear second-hand.'

'Of course, boss, but here's one more little nugget …' she hesitated, and it drove Hamilton nuts. 'Donna Moran graduated from Brunel University in the summer before her weekend away, which would have made her Class of 2015. Guess who else graduated that year?'

Hamilton slowly shook his head. 'Warren Speed?'

'Yup! I think it's safe to say we've found a link between the dead victim and the missing girl. I've also already got the list of names you want. They all made statements after Donna initially went missing.'

'The statements were made here, not in Ambleside?' he asked.

Fraser nodded, and Hamilton's mind went into overdrive. He wondered if the aloof Cumbrian Inspector would hand the case over to him, or at least share it, as there was a clear and direct connection with London. Despite wanting to jump on the phone and make demands of the coffee-drinking snob, Hamilton knew he would have to go through the proper channels. He glanced at the clock, and knowing his boss, Detective Chief Inspector Allen, wouldn't be in the building yet, he tried to control his haste.

'Let's be clever with this,' he said, rubbing his index finger over his lip. 'Before another major case load attacks us, let's simmer with this and see what else we can establish before I talk to the Chief.'

'Sure thing,' she said and scooped her long locks into a messy bun. 'How was your impromptu escape … before the arrival of a dead body, of course.'

'It was great, thanks. Lovely to see my mum. The countryside really suits her. Hey, what about your cat?' he asked, remembering a conversation they'd shared when he invited the team to a BBQ at his house the previous weekend.

Fraser's pink lips turned down. 'He still hasn't been home. I'm actually beginning to think someone stole him.'

'What makes you say that?'

She hesitated, and the quietness was quickly replaced with the laughter of Clarke and Rocky as they entered the office. 'Could we talk about this another time, boss?' Fraser said. 'There is actually something I'd like to discuss with you anyway.'

'Sure, whenever you want, I'm here. You know that,' Hamilton replied and turned to greet his colleagues.

'Alright, gov, good weekend?' his partner, Detective Sergeant Lewis Clarke, asked.

'In a word … interesting, that's for sure. Fraser tells me you've had a pretty nasty case to deal with?'

'Well, the show does go on, even when you're not here.'

For nearly five years, they'd worked together in the murder investigations team, and Hamilton had become accustomed to Clarke's sarcastic tone. A bachelor, who prided himself on his appearance, Hamilton had never seen Clarke without a clean-shaven face and a considerable amount of gel styling his black hair. He was an extrovert, and many times, Hamilton had watched his partner's blue eyes come alive when conversing with a pretty woman – even when swarmed by a medical team, after having been stabbed in the stomach by the last offender they'd arrested. But he was a good detective, and that was all that mattered to Hamilton.

'Where's Dixon?' he asked, glancing around the room.

'She'll be about an hour late this morning,' Rocky informed him in his diluted Irish accent. 'Something to do with the kids, but she didn't really go into specifics, sir.'

Hamilton liked Rocky, professionally known as Detective Constable Robbie O'Connor, and admired the lad's laid-back approach to life. Given the nickname Rocky because of his initials and sparring hobby, he'd left Ireland as a teenager to pursue a career in the force, and Hamilton sensed a spark from deep within the new recruit. He'd transferred to their team as a rookie almost two weeks before, and had hit the ground running. Embracing his promotion, Rocky dealt with the upheaval of moving to London from Hertfordshire and adjusted to the capital's rent increase in one week. Coupled with finalising a divorce in his early thirties, it couldn't be easy, Hamilton imagined, and many people might have lost their fiery sprit. But Rocky's cheeky grin, and the sparkle in his hazel eyes, had never faltered.

Although he had only scraped the surface of Rocky's story, he knew the lad was a hard worker – a non-negotiable trait for Hamilton. However, it was DS Yasmine Dixon he'd yet to grasp professionally, joining the team just days before his last-minute holiday to Ambleside. Creating a dedicated murder investigations team was his top priority, and the need to understand each colleague was of the utmost importance. He frowned, while drumming his fingers on the desk, then shook away the feeling of uncertainty from his mind.

'Okay, no worries. I'll catch up with her whenever she gets in,' Hamilton finally replied. 'Fraser, can you bring these two up-to-date with what we've been working on? I want us to get out there and interview people connected to Donna Moran as soon as possible.'

'You've been back for about half an hour, and already *you're* updating *us*, gov,' Clarke teased.

'Like you said, partner, the show doesn't stop because I have a weekend off. I just make sure I'm never the last one off the starting block,' he replied, and clapped a hand on Clarke's back. 'Right, make yourselves familiar with this investigation. Hopefully, the Chief has some time to see me this morning … I want to steal a case from the Cumbria Constabulary.'

CHAPTER FIVE

Felicity Ireland exited the train and pulled at the pink, hummingbird patterned scarf strangling her. She took a moment to suck in the cool air, but was mindful to keep up the pace with the surrounding shoppers and students. The sunlight beamed in from the street, as she tapped her Oyster Card on the machine. The barriers automatically swung open, offering release from the darkness of the station.

Despite the groans of annoyance behind her, Felicity stopped and examined herself in the window of a closed-down shop, just feet before the exit. Although she had applied more foundation than ever before, it had done nothing to mask the ring of redness surrounding her swollen green eyes. She had pulled half of her blonde hair back with a clip, the irritation of it falling into her face beginning to grow by the day, but the waves still danced effortlessly around her shoulders. Her plain black shirt glided down her long, slender body and tucked neatly into her dark denim jeans, tan-coloured Chelsea boots matched the shade of her Michael Kors tote bag perfectly. The woman staring back from the blacked-out window looked like Felicity Ireland, but she certainly didn't feel herself.

She tugged at the pink material again, allowing the scarf to hang loosely around her neck, and watched her fingers mindlessly rubbing the edges between her thumb and fingers. It was a gift from Warren. They had celebrated their one-year anniversary in Mexico, a surprise, week-long trip he'd organised for her. Warren had called Felicity his hummingbird, because she was full of energy and colour … and her insane ability to hear anything he said, even if he whispered it from the next room. It had been the happiest time of her life, until Warren had proposed, and filled her with joy once again. A small smile spread across her sad face, and she hated herself for allowing a moment of happiness to slip through. Emotions from the past and present mixed inside her like lava waiting to erupt. The confusion of everything that had happened in the last few months stung, and she wondered if she'd made the right decision coming here today.

An elbow jabbed into the small of her back and yanked Felicity from the shadows of her past. She was back in Uxbridge. The ear-deafening train announcements boomed from unseen speakers, the muffled chatter of strangers passing-by, and the sound of feet smacking the ground as people ran to make the next departure popped the bubble she'd been lost in. She inhaled deeply, grabbed the wide-rimmed sunglasses from her bag, and turned to brave the light. And her friends.

As usual, the street was crowded with people, despite it being a weekday. Cars waited impatiently as students strolled along the cobbled paving with no sense of urgency. Felicity smiled again, thinking back to the days she would have ambled along those very streets, probably missing a lecture, and deciding which venue to drink at that night. The men on the stalls yelled for attention, boasting about their seasonal goods; today's offerings were strawberries. Felicity could see the entrances to both shopping centres – Intu Uxbridge on her left and The Pavillions across the road to her right. But it was the coffee shop a few yards away from the station she was interested in. She spotted her friends straight away, sitting outside around a rickety, metal table. She frowned when counting four chairs were occupied, rather than the three she'd been expecting.

During their three years at university, Todd, Calvin, and Holly were Felicity and Warren's closest friends. Within days of meeting each other during fresher's week, they had formed an unbreakable bond which had lasted through every high and low of their degrees; failing grades, or failing relationships, new opportunities and new jobs, they supported each other.

Felicity swallowed back the tears and lifted her head high as she walked towards them. Butterflies danced in her stomach as she approached what felt like four strangers.

Holly was the first out of her seat, repeating the word "sorry," while wrapping her arms tightly around Felicity's neck. Her cropped, red hair came as a shock, and Felicity couldn't decide if the sharp style suited her friend's round face and curvaceous frame. But it wasn't the time to make comments like that.

'I'm so glad you contacted us,' Holly mumbled into her ear. 'I didn't know what to do.'

Calvin stood and hovered awkwardly. Felicity gently rubbed his arm, giving him permission to sit back down. He'd never been comfortable with public displays of affection. Todd merely sat, playing with the empty sugar packet next to his coffee cup, and Felicity waited for eye contact When he eventually raised his sea blue eyes, she lightly grinned, and he mirrored her expression. The real stranger at the table coughed, jolting Felicity from her trance, and forcing her to look at the woman.

'Sorry, this is Mel,' Todd said, his cockney accent always carried a smoothness with it. It wasn't harsh and abrupt; it was warm and hypnotic. 'We're kinda … seeing each other. A few months now. But she was dying to meet you all. Shit! Sorry, I shouldn't have said dy–'

'It's fine,' Felicity interrupted sharply and held out her hand to Mel. 'It's lovely to meet a new friend of Todd's. I'm glad you could join us.'

Her statement couldn't have been farther from the truth. Her stomach clenched as she took her seat, glancing at the beautiful blonde across the table. Everything was perfect. From the woman's sun-kissed skin and pearly white teeth, to her muscular arms and perky breasts – which Felicity was sure wouldn't drop an inch even after the padded bra was removed. The woman reminded her of Jennifer Aniston. However, that wasn't the reason she was unwelcome, and any other day she would have been more interested in this yoga-toned goddess. Today's out-of-the-blue meeting was about confronting her friends. She needed to see their reactions. She needed to know their thoughts.

Despite not being the first time they'd met since graduating two years ago, Felicity's stomach somersaulted, as if she were dauntingly making new friends in the school playground. On occasion, they had gravitated back together and sat at the very same table, but it'd been all fake smiles and small talk. Warren could never understand why she bothered, and he was always too busy to attend, but the others all had their reasons: guilt, boredom, curiosity. For Felicity, she missed the bond they'd shared at one point in their lives. The hysterical laughter, collective hopes and dreams, and a genuine passion for life. She wondered, if they continued to meet, could they someday bury their secrets, and return to how they'd been before?

'How are you holding up?' Holly finally broke the silence. 'I couldn't believe it when I saw your WhatsApp pop up on the group message.'

'I couldn't just sit around, doing nothing and waiting for answers. It's not what Warren would have wanted. It's not the type of person I am.'

'He would have wanted you to be safe.'

Felicity frowned and glanced around the table at her friends, skimming over new-girl Mel, whose incessant chewing on a chocolate twist made her want to scream. She remained silent for a few moments and thought, could they all be thinking exactly the same thing as she was?

'I'm not stupid ...' she replied. 'Warren was murdered on the anniversary of Donna's disappearance. At the same spot, we –'

'Shut up!' Calvin roared, attracting the attention from customers at a few other tables. 'For fuck's sake, we don't know her,' he said, pointing at Mel.

Felicity watched his brow furrow deeper into his dark skin. He lowered his finger and roughly rubbed his hand back and forth over his neat cornrows. Calvin wasn't much of a talker, though it was hard to be when Warren had usually held everyone's attention. But Calvin could be quick-witted, and Felicity always enjoyed his dry sense of humour. It was rare to see him worked up, like now; his large chest rose and fell at a rate of knots, and a twitch in his jaw became evident.

'Chill out, mate,' Todd replied and placed his hand on Mel's crossed thighs. 'She's cool. I've told her everything. You don't need to be secretive around her.'

'Well, she shouldn't know *everything*,' Calvin retorted through gritted teeth.

As much as Felicity didn't welcome the company of the newcomer, she had to support Todd. It was actually comforting to see him in a relationship after years of living the bachelor life. She didn't want Mel scared off, which could, in turn, take their friend away from them too.

'Come on, Calvin,' she said light-heartedly. 'Anyone can do a Google search and find a wealth of information about whomever they choose to these days. If Todd trusts her, then we should.'

The tension in Calvin's shoulders eased as he relaxed back into the plastic chair, but she couldn't help noticing the juddering of his right leg under the table. She exchanged glances with Mel, and the woman smiled sweetly. It made her feel good about herself for a few seconds, until Holly dragged her back to the dark reality of their meeting.

'Flick, do you want to talk about Warren? It's as clear as mud in the news article,' her friend said, shaking the long side of her fringe from her eyes – an annoying trait she'd always had, Felicity thought.

The use of her nickname pulled at her heart and flooded her mind with memories of better times. The six of them, thick as thieves, patrolling the grounds of Brunel University like they owned every building and had private shares in the student union. Their nights out at the campus bar or nightclub, dancing the night away, and stopping for chicken and chips before heading back to their halls of residence. Her five friends were the only ones who'd ever called her Flick, and she had always wondered why no-one at primary school, or college, or even at home had. It seemed so natural. She couldn't remember which member of their group had started the nickname, but it stuck. Warren, however, stopped using it two years ago, when all their lives had changed. He wanted to get away from the past more than anyone, and that meant only ever calling her "Felicity."

'Warren had been a bit … strange lately,' she confessed.

'Stranger than normal?' Todd mocked.

Felicity tutted and told him to keep quiet. 'Anyway … I think he was hiding something from me. A letter came in the post, and he put his defences up, not long after we announced our engagement.'

'Do you know who it was from?' Holly asked.

She hesitated for a few moments, debating whether or not to tell her friends the truth. As much as Warren loved to be in the limelight, for the cameras to be following his every move, she knew there were some things she shouldn't be sharing right now.

'No,' she finally answered.

'Maybe his personal assistant would know more?'

Felicity's head snapped up, her eyes glaring wide at Holly. 'What makes you think that?'

'Erm … didn't she arrange everything like that for him? She was with him every day.'

'So was I! I'm his fiancée. I mean … *was* …'

Holly reached over the table and took Felicity's hand. 'I'm sorry, I didn't mean to upset you. I just meant … I'm sure he made her sort all his letters and documents and … I'm sorry.'

Felicity shook her head, dismissing Holly's apology, and wiped the tears away, feeling idiotic as she did. Perhaps it was too soon to be faced with people and their opinions.

'Oh, I remember. She's the hot blonde one, right?' Todd laughed, as Mel punched him in the arm. 'I'm kidding, babe. I've only got eyes for you.'

He leant over and gave the attractive woman a lingering kiss. Felicity had to look away. Not out of jealously or bitterness, but she'd caught sight of how Mel looked at Todd. There was evident lust; there always was in the early stages of a relationship, but she also hung on his every word. When he moved, Mel moved. Felicity could see now. It was exactly how she and Warren would act. She missed the expert touch of his fingers on her bare legs. His piercing blue eyes could swallow her like the torrential waves of the ocean.

'When's the funeral?' Calvin blurted, and Todd jabbed him in the ribs.

'I'm not sure,' Felicity replied quietly. 'The police haven't released his body.'

'He's still in Ambleside?' her friend continued to question.

'Yes. I'm not sure, I haven't been given all the information, but, for some reason, the Met are involved in this too. His body may be transferred to their morgue after the post-mortem.'

Todd grabbed Mel's packet of cigarettes, handed his girlfriend one, and took one for himself. He ignored her offer of a lighter and drummed the white tobacco stick on the table.

'What the hell was he doing there?' he exclaimed, looking at no one in particular, before lighting the cigarette and taking a long drag from the tip.

They were all used to Todd's habit, and had long since stopped telling him the dangers of it. Felicity wafted the smoke away from her face, the attack of fumes doubled now two chimneys sat around the table. Todd's question repeated over and over in her mind. She couldn't stand not knowing, and the vagueness of everything surrounding the murder of her fiancée. Not for the first time since the police had knocked at her door, she wanted to scream. The frustration was eating away at her. The smoke blurred the faces in front of her.

'I don't know, but I'm going to find out,' Felicity said and slowly looked around the table, holding eye contact with each one of them for a few seconds. 'We're all going to find out. And I think we need to start by telling the truth about what happened two years ago.'

Later that night, when Felicity had wiped away the layers of make-up and shed herself of the labels, she curled up on her lonely double bed. She clung to Warren's pillow, breathing in the faint smell of his DKNY aftershave lingering on the material, and cried herself to sleep. The agony of losing her best friend, her soulmate and her lover ripped at her heart until she felt nothing.

CHAPTER SIX

Hamilton's feet pounded the pavement as he raced through the bustling crowd of Leicester Square. Despite Rocky clearing a path ahead of him, the mob of tourists and popular caricaturists was never ending. Barging shoulders, knocking shopping bags, and hopping over small children like a hurdle jumper, he'd expertly avoided the street bollards. Except the last one, hidden behind a family taking a group shot outside the M&M store. Hamilton swerved around them, but dashed directly into the thick, steel post, grinding him to painful halt.

'Why do they always have to bloody run?' he muttered, doubling over and clutching his crown jewels. 'And why do I never jump back in the car to give chase?'

He stretched up, grimacing as he did, and slowly swirled around. He'd lost his bearings and couldn't see Rocky, or the suspect, running away in any direction. Amidst the dazzling lights of the huge buildings, and serenity of the near-by greenery and Shakespeare fountain, Hamilton inhaled deeply. The pride he felt when calling this picturesque London town his home sometimes overwhelmed him.

Hamilton decided to return to the car, and walking through Cecil Court, his mind briefly wandered to Elizabeth. Christmas was less than six months away, and his wife read books like they were going out of fashion. He made a mental note to come back to this array of book shops on his next rest day. As he turned right on to St Martin's Lane, where they'd parked the car less than twenty minutes earlier, he whistled aloud. Rocky leant casually against his silver Vauxhall Corsa outside Gymbox. The lad stood to attention immediately and frowned when he noticed Hamilton's limp.

'I'm fine,' he said, waving away Rocky's concern. 'It's just my pride that's dented. I'm sure you understand. Given me the slip too.'

Rocky made a clicking noise with his tongue and thumbed in the direction of the car window. 'Got our guy, sir. Thought he'd lost us and tried to double back. I might have a heavy build, but it's muscle not fat, and I'm a fast runner.'

Hamilton couldn't contain his smile. 'Well, for someone who's still learning the winding, busy streets of London, I'm impressed.' He took the keys from Rocky and walked around the car. 'Oh, and I think it's time you stopped calling me "sir." It's an old-fashioned title that makes me feel ancient. And no more jumping to attention when you see me. Yes, I'm your superior, and most of the time, I'll give the orders, but we're a team.'

'Good to know, sir … sorry, I mean, gov.' Rocky climbed in the passenger's seat. 'You didn't do too bad back there. I'm looking for a new gym to join in London. You'd be more than welcome to join me. I could help you work on your core muscles and speed.'

Hamilton laughed out loud and started the engine. 'Let's mark that down as a maybe for now, Rocky.'

'This ain't fair! I can't fucking be treated like this,' a gruff voice roared from the back of the car.

'Did you read the man his rights, DC O'Connor?'

'Yes, DI Hamilton. First thing I did, after pinning him to the ground to stop him escaping again, of course.'

'Of course,' he echoed.

Hamilton sniffed, mockingly taking his time as he allowed pedestrians to cross the road, before turning onto William IV Street. Despite Charing Cross Police Station being situated just yards away, so close in fact they could have walked, Hamilton was training his new recruit. He needed Rocky accustomed with London's vibrant roads before going out in the field alone.

'Well then, you should know running away from us was a pretty stupid thing to do,' Hamilton finally said and peered into the rear-view mirror.

The man's face was freshly shaven, and he could have easily passed as a teenager. Especially with his fashion choice of a black Yankees cap, which he pulled further over his dark eyes when he caught Hamilton's gaze.

'I ain't done nothing wrong! This is racism. Bullying. A black man can't walk around London without the pigs thinking he's done something wrong. And from you too, fella, a copper of colour. I'd expect more loyalty from you,' the man said, jabbing his finger in Hamilton's direction.

The car came to an abrupt stop directly outside the station. Hamilton parallel parked into a tight spot with ease, ignoring the man sitting in the back, who continued to mouth off about equality and race. Before he released the detainee from the car, he called Rocky to one side.

'Don't waste your breath on him once we're inside. We'll get the desk sergeant to book him in, and he can wallow for a while.'

'You don't want to interview him straight away, gov?' Rocky frowned.

'No. I can't handle loud mouths like him. He's under suspicion, he's been cautioned, and he's a flight risk. An hour in a confined space won't do any harm. Might actually shut him up for when I'm finally ready for him.'

'Your call, gov.'

The man continued to swear, yell, and fight against Hamilton and Rocky as they yanked him from the car. Although he had no choice in the final destination, it was clear he wasn't going to enter the building quietly. Regardless of the fact the man's wrists were handcuffed, Hamilton gripped his arms just that bit tighter than he normally would.

'You really are a prize prat, aren't you?' Hamilton muttered into the man's ear, as they dragged him up the steps and through the main door. 'We only wanted to ask you a few questions … for your help, really. Now, I couldn't be more suspicious of you.'

He felt the man's shoulders slump, the struggle ceased, and quietness resumed. Hamilton grinned and shook his head. *How predictable*, he thought.

* * *

'For the benefit of the tape, Calvin Robinson has declined the offer to have a solicitor present,' Hamilton said an hour later, when he began the interview. 'Why did you run from us, Mr Robinson?'

The man, slouched in the chair as though he was waiting for a movie to start, simply shrugged his shoulders and continued to stare at the table.

Hamilton couldn't work it out. The man was a potential witness. A friend of the missing girl, who, by coincidence, worked closest to the station and was therefore their first port of call. He could understand people instinctively felt nervous when a police car cruised behind them in slow traffic or approached them on the street. But to run from your place of work, before enquiring as to why they were there, sounded alarm bells in his head.

'Do you want to explain why you ran when we entered the coffee shop and asked for you?' he continued.

Calvin rubbed a hand over his tightly plaited hair and sat up straight. Hamilton glimpsed something, a look of wretchedness in the man's eyes, and for the first time, the red glare around his pupils.

'I don't know. Guess I haven't had the best of experiences with you pi … with you coppers,' Calvin replied and returned his gaze to the large metal furniture separating them.

Hamilton cursed himself for not delving further into this guy's record. But then, he hadn't previously noticed the bloodshot eyes, and he hadn't planned on interrogating him.

'Mr Robinson, are you on drugs?'

'What?' the man screeched, a little too high-pitched for Hamilton's liking.

'You know, drugs that make you a little wavy. Marijuana, weed, sunk … whatever it is you guys smoke these days.' He raised his eyebrows. 'What are you, twenty-four? Think that crap is going to help you get anywhere in life?'

Calvin sighed and folded his arms across his broad chest, the black T-shirt stretching tighter over his large muscles. They were getting nowhere. Frustrated, he decided to question the man about what really interested him right now.

'Look, Calvin, this has all blown out of proportion. You don't trust the police, that much is obvious. But we were seriously just coming around for a friendly chat. It wasn't even about you … not directly.' He had the man's attention once again. 'We're trying to get some information on a young woman, Donna Moran.'

Hamilton watched Calvin's reaction as he said the name. The way his Adam's apple protruded a centimetre more as he gulped. His knee, jittering under the table, and the way his eyes darted between Hamilton and Rocky.

'I … don't know,' the man stuttered.

'Don't know what, Mr Robinson? Who she is, or where she is?'

'Well, no. I mean … yes.'

'Yes, you do know Donna Moran, and you know where she is?'

'I didn't say that.'

'You said no, then yes. So, what does that mean? Do you know where Donna Moran is?'

Calvin slammed his fist on the table, but the rest of his body stiffened.

Hamilton folded his arms on the table and slid in closer. Inches from the man's face, he repeated his question. 'Mr Robinson, do you know the whereabouts of Donna Moran?'

'No.'

'Do you *know* Donna Moran?'

'Yes.'

Hamilton sat back in his chair, watching Calvin's dry tongue attempt to moisten his even drier lips. He let the silence simmer in the thick air for a few moments longer. The man was over a decade younger than him; a boy, in Hamilton's opinion. But as Calvin sat there, with a temper somewhere between blasé and fury, he knew this *boy* had important information. The tiny droplets of sweat, brimming at the top of his forehead, was just one of the tell-tale signs an inspector with over fifteen years' service wouldn't miss.

'DC O'Connor, can you get Mr Robinson a strong coffee, please? I think there's something significant he needs to share with us.'

CHAPTER SEVEN

'Chief come on. Surely you can see this is a Met case, regardless of where the crime scene is. It needs to be transferred over to us,' Hamilton almost yelled at his superior. 'The links to London are obvious. I'm sure even Inspector Ray Bennett will understand that.'

DCI Allen rested back into the office chair, folded his large, muscular arms over his chest, and clamped his fingers together. He had achieved his position with the backing of everyone he'd worked with; a fair boss, who supported his colleagues but had no time for insubordination. Growing up in Cork as a six-foot tall brute, he'd learnt to defend himself and speak up for those weaker than him. By the age of twenty, he knew the career path he wanted to take and headed for London. Now, despite knocking on the door of his sixtieth birthday, and the grey hairs outnumbering the black, it was clear the man still felt that same fire of his youth; everyone deserved justice.

'I can understand why you want to reopen the Donna Moran case, Denis,' Allen finally said. 'As a potential victim and witness, I'll let you and your team have that. But we cannot demand the local police of Ambleside hand over a murder which took place in their own backyard.'

'What if I speak to Bennett, try and appeal to his better nature?' Hamilton pleaded, wondering if the local man had one at all. 'They would still be involved in the case, of course, I'd ensure that.'

Allen groaned. 'Maybe … The force won't want the extra expense of their officers travelling back and forth.'

'In this day and age, sir? No, we can … Skype, if they have to physically see us. I'll keep them in the loop with anything we find, as I'm sure they will us. They still have Warren Speed's body, after all.'

The Chief laughed out loud. 'I see your team are having an influence on you, Denis.'

He rolled his eyes and held up his hands. 'What can I say? It's all video conferencing and technology these days. But, yes, they are teaching me a thing or two.'

'Who says you can't teach an old dog new tricks, hey?'

There was a spark in Allen's eyes, and the hopeful feeling rose in Hamilton. He couldn't pinpoint the exact reason he pushed for the case; maybe because he'd been at the lake the day the body had been discovered, or because his heart went out to the mother who had no clue where her daughter was. Unsure as he was, he wasn't prepared to give up.

'So, what do you reckon, Chief?'

Allen sighed heavily and sat forward, his large physique overshadowing the oak desk. 'I think it's better I support you with this, because I have a feeling you'd go off behind my back anyway. Start with Donna Moran, for now. Let's see if we can discount her as a potential victim. I have a contact in Ambleside, so leave that side of things with me for the time being. The press is having a field day with this Warren Speed case, so it might be in the Met's interest to be involved, or at least have a finger in the proverbial pie.'

'Cheers, sir. I appreciate your backing,' Hamilton said and raced from the office.

On his return to the incident room, he was pleased to see the newest member of the team, DS Yasmine Dixon, had joined them.

'Inspector Hamilton, I'm being bought up to speed right now, and I'll work late to make up the time,' she blurted out.

Hamilton raised a hand, hoping to slow her down. 'I know we all have a life outside of this office, Dixon. Don't get in such a panic over it. Are your kids okay?'

'They're fine. It's the final week of the summer holidays, and things get a bit out of control with dance clubs and football practice and dentist appointments,' Dixon explained and pulled her long, dark hair away from her slim, golden-brown face. 'My husband is with them now, so he can deal with it. Jeez, couldn't you just wring their necks sometimes.'

Hamilton smiled, but noticed the aghast expressions spread across Clarke and Fraser's faces. Dixon's hand flew to her mouth, and the room suddenly lacked any fresh air, despite the wide-open windows. He knew no-one would speak first, all waiting on him, and difficult relationships between his new team members was the last thing they needed.

'Hey, we all need to rant somewhere, right? We're here for that … anything you need to guarantee you aren't *really* wringing anyone's neck when you leave this building.'

Clarke was the first to slice through the thick atmosphere with a hearty laugh, and Hamilton was thankful for it. Dixon obviously knew about Maggie, and while that fact didn't bother him, the thought of colleagues walking on eggshells around him again did. It had been five years; people had the right to talk about their children freely in front of him.

He clapped his hands and undid whatever spell had mesmerised them for a few moments. The blush eased from Dixon's face, and he was eager to pull them all back to the task.

'Now, talking of children, there's a mother out there who hasn't heard from her daughter in two years,' he said.

Clarke perched on the desk. 'Well, that's what we *think*, gov.'

'Yes, you've got a point. Fraser, did you manage to contact Joan Moran?'

She grimaced. "Sorry, boss, not yet. It's the next thing to do on my list.'

'It should have been actioned already,' he snapped. 'Even as a courtesy, the woman needs to be informed her daughter's case has been reopened. When you speak to her, don't mention the note extracted from Warren Speed's mouth just yet. Explain we've reopened it as the anniversary has recently passed. Find out if she's spoken to Donna, or her friends, or has any other information.'

'Will do, boss. I have her contact details. I'll see if she'll have a chat with me over the phone first,' Fraser said.

Hamilton nodded, grabbed a black marker and wrote notes on the white evidence board as he spoke. 'Unfortunately, the details Calvin Robinson gave us were not as interesting as I'd hoped. It was pretty much what he'd said two years ago, but there was something about him … I don't know. Plus, his is only one side of the story, and there were six people involved that weekend. One of those is missing, and another one's been murdered. What I suggest we do is split up and interview the three remaining friends who were on the Lake Windermere trip. See if they have any fresh material we can work with.'

'Gov, why don't we just get the four of them in a room together and see what they have to say?' Rocky suggested.

'What do you think this is, an episode of Poirot?' Hamilton said sarcastically, and heard a snigger from Dixon. He wondered if the joke was wasted on the younger three of the team. 'By tackling them individually, they're more likely to tell us something they wouldn't in the company of their friends. Maybe even slip up and confess something they omitted from their original statements.'

Rocky didn't flush red at Hamilton's comment. Instead, he smiled with the rest of them and hitched up his shoulder. 'Okay, I understand. Remember, I'm learning from you every day.' The twinkle in Rocky's eye shone as blatantly as his tongue-in-cheek tone.

'What did the Chief have to say?' Clarke asked.

'He thinks the fact Donna Moran's name was literally dragged from the corpse of her friend gives us some scope to be involved. Like me, he also believes she could be in danger. Possibly even the next victim.'

'Or she's the murderer,' Dixon added, placing her hands on her petite hips. 'It could be her calling card, informing the authorities she's thought about this for some time. Wants everyone to know she's taken revenge.'

'Revenge for what?' Rocky asked.

Dixon shrugged. 'That's why we need to find her.'

Hamilton mulled the idea over. 'It's not the conclusion I came to, only because I saw the size of Warren Speed, and the fact he'd been placed in the Lake and tied up.'

'Maybe she wasn't alone.' Rocky clicked his fingers.

Hamilton continued writing all the possibilities on the white board, as the team fired their differing theories back and forth.

'I like this,' he said, 'but it's all speculation at the moment. Which is only urging me on to find Donna Moran and get some real facts. We have to remember, the other four people in this friendship could be in danger also.'

'Where's Calvin Robinson now?' Clarke asked.

'Officially, we had no reason to keep him here, or put a tail on him. Despite there being something off about the lad, and the fact he's definitely dabbling in some kind of narcotics, his pockets were empty. We'll keep an eye on him, though, maybe through his movements on social media, Fraser?'

She nodded and quickly scribbled herself a note. 'Also, boss, I couldn't remember if I told you this already, but not only is Felicity Ireland the fiancée of Warren Speed, she's also one of the friends who was on the getaway with Donna.'

'Right, Dixon and I will go and have a chat with her. Clarke and Rocky, you take one of the others on the list each, and whoever finishes first can visit the last witness,' Hamilton informed them.

If the swap in partners jarred Clarke, he didn't bring any attention to the fact. Retrieving the contact details from Fraser's desk, he left the office. Hamilton made a mental note to touch base with him later, just in case. For now, he needed to get to know Dixon more, and for him, this was the only way he knew how, other than unashamedly interrogating the poor woman.

* * *

Hamilton gazed up at the tall, mirrored windows of the office block in Euston, just twenty minutes after leaving the station. The drive had been surprisingly quiet, and although he'd planned to use the time to get to know Dixon more, something held him back. It wasn't her obvious beauty, or athletic figure – ogling wasn't his style – he hadn't looked at another woman in *that* way since he'd met Elizabeth. Plus, he'd always preferred the fuller figure anyway. He assumed her earlier child-beating comment was at fault and decided to wait until she felt more comfortable with him before he started prying.

'So, Felicity Ireland is a journalist. Interesting,' Dixon commented, as they entered the building for *Today's News*.

'Not exactly your national coverage, but she could have friends in high places.'

'You think she could have leaked the details about Warren Speed's death?'

He sighed and waited for the woman at reception to acknowledge them. 'Who knows the inner workings of a journalist's mind. I've never had a great relationship with the press.'

After the introductions were made, Hamilton and Dixon were given the directions to Miss Ireland's office. Surprised that the young lady, whose name tag read Fleur, didn't escort them personally, he determined it must be an informal building. They took the lift to the third floor and stepped out into a large, open-plan office. No one bothered to look up from their work stations, either too busy drumming on their keyboards or having phone conversations. Various personal offices were situated around the side, most with the doors closed. He located the plaque he wanted: *Felicity Ireland, Editorial Assistant.*

He took a minute to watch the woman. Her wavy blonde hair fell around her porcelain face and swished on her shoulders as she moved between the laptop and files; nothing seemingly held her attention for long. When she glanced up, he recognised the look of melancholy in her bloodshot eyes, shadowed by the dark circles of sleep deprivation.

'Hello, Miss Ireland. My name is Detective Inspector Hamilton, and this is Detective Sergeant Dixon. Could we come in and speak to you for a few moments, please?'

She closed a brochure containing a collage of wreath selections, and placed it into a drawer of the black desk. Far from a grand room, with its basic furniture and office supplies, it gained points for its picturesque view of Euston Square Gardens. The woman stood out in this plain office, Hamilton thought, dressed smarter than those outside in the open-planned office; a pink scarf hung loosely around her neck, falling onto a navy blazer and white shirt combo.

'Of course, please take a seat,' Felicity said and outstretched her hand to the two chairs in front of her. 'Is this about Warren?'

'Not directly. The Cumbria Constabulary are still processing the evidence. We're here to ask you about Donna Moran.'

Felicity's eyes widened for just a second, before she relaxed back into the chair, but the flush of red rising along her cheeks piqued Hamilton's interest.

'Really, why?' she asked.

'We've reopened Donna Moran's missing person's file and are visiting everyone who made an original statement after her disappearance.'

Dixon edged closer and casually leaned on the table, her black notebook and pen rested on her knee, out of sight. Felicity reached for a corner of her scarf and idly rubbed it between her fingers.

'I don't have anything to add to my original statement, Inspector,' Felicity said. 'I'm sorry, but nothing's changed since I spoke to the police two years ago.'

Hamilton smiled and bridged his hands over his stomach. 'Humour me, Miss Ireland. I've read a few reports, but I like to get a gist of things for myself. Just start from the beginning.'

He noted the woman's slight eye roll, but she pulled her blazer closer across her chest and sat forward.

'Donna and I were friends while we studied at Brunel University. We met during fresher's week, when we first arrived, and developed a close bond over the following three years.' She looked down. 'We were good friends.'

'And the weekend she went missing … you were on some kind of trip, is that correct?'

Felicity bit on her lower lip and made eye contact with him again. 'Yes. We graduated the same year and decided a cheeky weekend away to celebrate was what we all needed. I found a great offer on Groupon, and we visited Ambleside. The night before we were due to travel back to London …' she said hesitantly.

Not wanting to interrupt her flow, Hamilton and Dixon remained quiet.

'Donna was a bit … weird. She wouldn't tell us what was going on, but decided to go for a walk. She never came back.'

'So, you just decided to leave the Lake District without her?' Dixon asked, and Hamilton smiled internally. His colleague's tone appeared light, but the question forceful.

'No, not all,' Felicity exclaimed. 'When we went to her room the following morning, her bag was gone, and she'd left a note. It said … she just wanted to get home, and that she'd already left. Except when we finally arrived back in London, her mum said she hadn't seen or heard from her. I tried to call … but it kept going to voicemail. Mrs Moran said we had to make a statement to the police, report Donna missing. But your guys didn't help much, because Donna was twenty-one and had left of her own free will.'

Hamilton sat forward and nodded in reply to Felicity's final defensive comment. 'And who is this "we" you've mentioned? Could you give us the names of those on the trip with you?'

'I'm confident you have all this information, Inspector.'

He smiled and raised his eyebrows.

'Fine! Other than myself and Donna, Warren, Todd Bell, Holly Walker, and Calvin Robinson.'

'Ah, yes, we've already spoken to Mr Robinson.' Hamilton waited for a reaction, but Felicity's expression remained unchanged. 'Have you, or any of your friends, heard from Donna at all in the past two years?'

'No, nothing.' She gazed at the mounds of paperwork on her desk, and her focus seemed to slip away while she spoke. 'For a while, after that weekend, I would check Twitter and Facebook every single day. I guess I was hoping she'd post *something*, even a photograph to let us know she was okay. But nothing ever came. She just vanished.'

'You mentioned Donna's mood being a bit off the last time you saw her,' Dixon said. 'Could she have had an argument with anyone, either someone at Ambleside or back in London? A boyfriend, perhaps?'

Felicity gently shook herself back to the present. 'I don't know. Donna was kind of seeing Warren at the time.'

Dixon and Hamilton exchanged glances. 'That wasn't mentioned in any of the original statements,' he said.

'Why would it have been? They fooled around for a bit. It wasn't anything serious. Everyone has a bit of fun while they're at uni. And they definitely didn't have a fight, or anything like that, while we were away.'

'When did you and Warren begin dating, Miss Ireland?' Hamilton continued.

Her eyes glistened. She clenched her jaw while brushing the tears away. 'About five or six months after … after Donna ran away. It was New Year's Eve, and we'd grown even closer than before … comforted each other. We just couldn't comprehend why Donna would run away, without a word to us. We had all been so close. Anyway, that night, we made a promise to each other to move on with our lives. Now … Warren's gone, and I don't … understand.' Felicity caught the falling teardrops with a tissue she grabbed from a box on the table. 'Why are you asking me these questions? Is Donna involved with Warren's murder? That's why you're asking about their relationship now, after all this time. Have you finally found her?'

'No, Miss Ireland, we haven't found Donna. But we are making an effort to do so. I think we'll leave it there, for now,' Hamilton said and stood up. 'Here's my card. If there's anything you can think of to help –'

'Now you're looking for her?' Felicity roared and jumped from her seat. 'Now that two years has passed. What about Warren? What about my fiancé? Who's looking for his murderer?'

'I can understand your frustrations and pain, Miss Ireland. Please know, your fiancé's case is being investigated.'

'He's just another case to you. But … he's a person. A person I loved. A human being …'

'Who was murdered in the same vicinity where you last saw your missing friend, Miss Ireland. We cannot ignore that fact.'

Despite Hamilton neglecting to inform Felicity of the handwritten note extracted from Warren's mouth, he hoped his stern tone opened her eyes to the severity of both investigations. Part of him wanted to warn her, but he didn't feel there was enough evidence in play, and the last thing he wanted was to ram fear into an already grieving woman. Or shake the murderer's resolve, causing them to flee before they had a chance to make an arrest. Felicity fell back into her chair and swivelled away from them. Facing the window, she dismissed them completely.

Exiting the building, something played on Hamilton's mind, an unnerving feeling rumbled in the pit of his stomach.

'Miss Ireland's version of events were the same as Mr Robinson's.'

Dixon lingered at the car door. 'Isn't that a good thing?'

'I mean, the same as in pretty much word-for-word. Like they were reading from a script. Feels a bit unnatural, especially after all this time.' He shook his head. 'Let's go and have a chat to the others, and see how we feel once we've gathered all of the statements.'

As Hamilton lowered himself to get in the car, a figure in his peripheral vision caught his attention. He snapped his head up, but the road was empty. Despite being parked on a side-street, he frowned at the quietness of a busy London area. As the engine roared to life, he shrugged it off, and his thoughts quickly returned to the case.

CHAPTER EIGHT

She slips the black, lace bra from her small, milky breasts. I can't take my eyes off her. It's not why I'm here, crouched in my hideout across the street, but now that I'm watching … I can't stop myself.

Do people really believe those wooden blinds protect their privacy? I can clearly see everything she's doing. Any prying eyes could, through those open slats. Why does no one around here feel the need to have net curtains, to shield the very windows into their homes? There were always net curtains hanging in the houses I grew up in … but, perhaps that says more about my trashy upbringing than it does about her.

I snap the twig I've been twiddling in my fingers and ball a fist. She's moved out of my view. I release the crumbled stick and reach for another, a larger one that won't break under the slightest pressure. I like to keep my hands busy when I follow her … which has become a regular occurrence over the last few weeks. A light from behind the frosted glass window in the bathroom illuminates her shadow, and my sigh of irritation transforms into a pleasurable groan. I can't see her body anymore, but I can imagine what she's doing.

Lately, she's distracted. For obvious reasons, I guess. But there's more playing on her mind … I know what she's like. The police have been hanging around, taking a particular interest in her, I think. I knew that mixed-raced copper would be a fucking problem. She's acting differently – there's a slump in her shoulders where she once walked tall with confidence. She's lost control, leaning on people, seeking their advice and guidance, which is very out of character for Miss Independent.

My thighs throb, so I stand slightly, still arched and concealed by the park trees and shrubbery. I think more about her change in character and wonder if it was always going to happen, eventually –no one can play that charade forever – or have my recent actions spiralled her into the unknown. Either way, perhaps this could be a blessing and work in my favour. Her unreliability is increasing … the twitchy nervousness she now exudes is undeniable. Surely, she'll tell the truth now. Surely, she'll have to confess.

An elderly man totters on the pavement in the direction of my hideout, so I squat back down, further into the bushes. The sniffing from his ugly dog is vociferous; on the other side of the wall, they walk closer and closer to me. I grab a large rock, prepare to smash it over the mongrel's head. The old man too, if need be. But I hear him call "Lucky" and grunt while impatiently pulling at the dog's lead.

Lucky, indeed.

It's time to make a decision. There's no denying I need to find out what happened that night, and I know I must stop hesitating. It won't be easy, but I owe it to myself. I owe it to her.

I take a deep breath, filling my nostrils with the dose of fresh air I need to push myself forward. Spluttering, I realise the mangy mutt took a shit on the other side of where I'm hiding. That's why the old man ran away so fast. My blood boils. Dog owners have no fucking respect for people who live around here, allowing their beasts to defecate wherever, fuck the consequences. I could have stepped in it when I climbed over the wall.

An empty, blue, plastic bag blows in the gentle wind, barely making it off the ground before it's caught by the bush. Where did it come from?

My anger subsides as an idea blossoms in my mind, as though the bag is a sign of what I must do next. I carefully creep over the wall, into the open street, my back to her house, and slide my hand into the plastic bag. I scoop up the hot lump of dog faeces, gag slightly, and tie a knot at the top of the bag.

I could use this against her. She's already worrying, on the verge of breaking down, perhaps I could speed things along. Push her over the edge, until she has no choice but to tell me everything I need to know. Give me everything I need to move on.

The annoying beep of a text message yanks me from my plan, and thrusts me back into the putrid reality I'm stuck in. I turn to see a figure on the other side of the street, outside her front gate, but engrossed with the mobile phone in their hand. I slip away, walking further up the street, but keep my eyes on her house for a few moments more.

Despite the shit swinging in my hand, I can't contain the vigorous whistle escaping my lips. Warren got off pretty lightly, when I think about it. Although I'd planned everything, it was rushed. I will not make that same mistake again.

CHAPTER NINE

Three years ago

The deep, rustic voice of Bryan Adams filled the dark bar. Felicity tipped her head forward, blonde curls flowing freely, as she imagined herself as the rocking guitar player on stage, and sang "Summer of '69" at the top of her voice. The multiple strobe lights ran over her hip-shaking body, as the solo instrument blared through the speakers, and she sashayed across the dance floor to her friends, who stood watching and laughing from the bar.

'It's the same every week,' Todd yelled over the music. 'How can you still have such enthusiasm for that song?'

Felicity guzzled down the remaining Snakebite from her pint glass and smiled. 'It reminds me of the night we all met during fresher's week. This club doesn't do anything better than Wednesday Cheese Nights, and I'll dance to it every week until I graduate.'

'I'm still surprised we met Calvin in here on a Wednesday night,' Holly said and refilled their pint glasses from the pitcher.

Calvin, the only one sat at the bar, shrunk further into the corner. 'I told you, I followed a hot blonde in here that night. Wish I hadn't now. I bloody hate this music. I only put up with it because of you lot.'

Holly tugged on Felicity's arm and jerked her head towards the end of the bar. 'I think someone's interested in your moves.'

She briefly peered at the spikey-haired guy wearing an England Rugby shirt and dark jeans. He flashed a smile, added a wink, and Felicity looked away.

'Nah, I'm fine on my own, Hols, but he's cute. You should go for it.'

Her friend shook her long, dark hair. 'He's not my type.'

Calvin groaned loudly. 'Do you see what I mean? What the hell is the DJ playing now?'

Felicity threw an arm in the air, posing like the Statue of Liberty, before jumping in with the song and singing, 'So hold on to the ones who really care, in the end they'll be the only ones there.' Then, she wrapped an arm around Todd and Holly's neck and continued to sing in Calvin's disapproving face.

'It's Hanson, "Mmmbop,"' Holly said, through bouts of laughter.

'For Christ's sake, shoot me now and get me out of here.' Calvin rolled his eyes and gulped from his pint.

'You can leave anytime you want, Cal, we're not forcing you to stay,' Felicity said, dropping the hold on her friends but continuing to dance. 'If you can't have a bit of fun and laugh at yourself every now and then, what's the point in life?'

He shouted something in reply about her lacking charm, but Felicity waved his comment away and walked through the sweaty crowd of dancing students. Since that first Wednesday during fresher's week, this had become her favourite night in the student union club. The drinks were cheap, the walk home minimal, and, most of all, people had a good time. There were never any untoward feelings or animosity when it came to dancing to cheesy records of the eighties and nineties. It was the one night of the week where Felicity unstrapped the responsibility and worry of everyday life, and really danced like no-one was watching.

Although desperate to make a stop at the toilet, the queue snaked out the door and along the wall. Felicity suddenly realised she hadn't seen Warren or Donna for a while and decided to hunt them down. On nights fuelled by alcohol, Warren would often give into the temptation of the smoking area, regularly encouraged by Todd, and so Felicity slipped through the doors of the nightclub and stepped out into the darkness of the night. She hadn't appreciated how much of sweat she'd worked up in there until the harshness of the wind slapped her across the face. Quickly glancing at the groups of people huddled in the cold, Felicity gave up and turned to go back in to the warmth.

A faint giggle came from the side of the building, just to the left of the entrance, and Felicity's curiosity got the better of her. She took a small side step and peered in the direction the laughter came from. She squinted in the shadows, but soon made out the two figures wrapped in a lust-hungry embrace. Their hands moved furiously over each other's bodies, pausing to undo a button or slip underneath a T-shirt. Felicity swallowed back the tears and turned to run, but slammed straight into a broad chest.

'Hey, where's the fire?' a familiar voice breathed in her ear.

'Nothing. I mean, nowhere. Let's get back inside, it's freezing out here,' she said but made no effort to move from the comfort of Todd's warm body.

He frowned and looked to where Felicity had been facing just moments before. She couldn't help but join him, and turned back just in time to see Warren and Donna slip further into the darkness, laughing as they pulled each other into the hidden shrubs and trees.

Calvin sighed heavily and ran a hand through his floppy, brown hair. 'That can't have been easy to see, Flick.'

'What are you talking about? We all knew it was going to happen.'

'Doesn't mean we all wanted it to happen,' he said softly, and placed his forefinger under her chin, lifting her face and forcing eye contact. 'You can do tons better than Warren Speed.'

'What if I don't want to?' she said, with immediate regret.

A lump rose in her throat, and the copious amounts of alcohol consumed hit home. Worried she wouldn't be able to keep the tears at bay, and desperate not to cry in front of Todd, she walked away. He grabbed her arm lightly, and she felt torn.

'I think your buzz has been killed for tonight,' he said and pulled her closer. 'It's okay, you know. I mean, I understand –'

'You understand nothing,' she interrupted. 'Because I don't care. We're all friends, and actually, if you think about it, all they're about to do is ruin the group dynamics.'

Todd swooped down and passionately kissed her. His large, warm hands cupped her face as his tongue slipped through her lips. Felicity returned the kiss, but her arms remained swinging by her side. She tugged away from his grasp and inhaled deeply.

'What the fuck are you doing, Todd?'

He stepped closer. 'Come on, you know how beautiful you are. Tonight, I couldn't take my eyes off your body, even dancing to cheesy tunes. You're amazing. Warren is a player … but me and you … that could be something.'

Felicity stood glaring at her friend for a few moments, the daze in her head now taking full effect. She didn't know what to say, or how she felt, and without thinking, her hand instinctively slapped Todd across the face.

'Jesus, Flick! That hurt.'

'I thought you were my friend,' she screamed.

He rubbed his cheek. 'I am your bloody friend … I just meant I thought it would be nice if we were *more* than that now.'

'When I first met you, in that first week, I told you I wasn't attracted to you. You said you understood, that you were cool being just mates. Are you telling me all this time … our friendship's been a lie?'

'Of course not. You're over-reacting. You mean the bloody world to me.'

The saliva deserted her dry mouth, and everything began spinning. '"I might not be able to have you as a girlfriend, but I certainly won't lose you as a friend." That's what you said to me last year.'

'And I meant it, woman! Calm down, it was just a kiss.'

'From one of my best friends.'

'I thought it was the right time. What with those two … you know.'

'What, shagging in the bushes?' she said with a frown, the pressure in her head now nauseating. 'I've told you, I don't care what they get up to. And it certainly doesn't mean I want to join them up against the wall with you, Todd. If you were truly my friend, you would have known that about me.'

Felicity ran away from the club, ignoring Todd, who shouted her name over and over again in the distance. She cringed as she pushed past Calvin and Holly, who had watched everything in silence from the entrance. She balled her hands into tight fists, hating the idea of being the butt of any joke, or rumour, especially between her closest friends. Staring at her feet as they gained momentum on the ground, she raced away with clouded thoughts, ignorant to everything else happening behind her.

CHAPTER TEN

Felicity grabbed the pink robe that hung on the back of her bedroom door and wrapped herself in it. Collapsing onto the bed, she buried her face in the soft towelling material and thought of Warren. Ironically, only now, everything she touched, saw, and smelt reminded her of him. She wondered if perhaps she'd dismissed work more often, and allowed her fiancé to enter her thoughts a bit more, perhaps she would know why he had returned to Lake Windermere.

After the police had left her office earlier that day, Felicity told her boss she wasn't ready to be back at work and rushed home. Everyone watched her, discussed her private life, and eyed her with suspicious glances. Some tipped their head sympathetically, while others probed with questions. She felt as though she was climbing a steep mountain in a thunderous downpour. She needed answers herself. The unknown was terrifying.

Before showering, and attempting to wash away the day's mental torture, Felicity called Warren's personal assistant. The woman didn't answer, and when the call immediately diverted to answerphone on the second attempt, she threw her iPhone across the bedroom. It bounced on the bed, but she didn't bother to check if it was still working. Strange, for a woman whose mobile seemed surgically attached to her hand. Was she past caring about everything so soon?

Felicity drew in a deep breath, but her body refused to rise from its horizontal position. Composing an email would be a wise decision, she thought. Claire could explain Warren's latest trip and help her understand why she wasn't aware of it before the police. But, even for a journalist, the words struggled to come together in coherent sentences, her mind as blank and empty as an artist's new canvas.

She lifted her head at the sound of her mobile's muffled vibrations. Retrieving her phone, she swung her feet over the edge of the bed and stared at her older sister's name flashing on the screen. Her thumb danced between the decline and answer buttons. The call stopped, but only for a few seconds. Felicity sighed at Dorinda's typical persistence, as the phone buzzed in her hand once again.

'Hey, you.'

'I called and called! Where have you been, Felicity?' her sister demanded. 'I phoned your office; they said you'd left early. That's so unlike you.'

The cracks in her resolve began to cave further. 'Are you serious?'

'Oh crap! I'm sorry … I didn't mean … Of course, things aren't normal right now. So, yes, you're not acting like yourself. I'm just worried about you.'

Felicity sniffed deeply, struggling to hold back the emotions bubbling at the surface. 'I know. It's okay … I know what you meant. I just couldn't handle the pitiful looks for much longer, the whispers in the offices, and how conversations stopped the minute I walked in.'

'Come on, sis, it's pretty big news. Everyone's talking about it.'

'I loved him. This is not a piece of gossip that will blow over in a day or two when something new comes along …'

'That's how you see it, because it's Warren. If it were anyone else, you'd probably be acting exactly the same as those tosspots. Maybe even trying to scope the story, or secure an interview yourself,' Dorinda said, in a matter-of-fact tone.

'Gosh … when you put it like that … I sound like a lovely person to be around, don't I?'

Dorinda giggled down the phone. Her sister wasn't being malicious or unfair in her observation. And as much as Felicity wanted to hate her for being brutally honest, when all she wanted was to be scooped up and held, it was impossible. Her sister was right.

'I feel awful, Dorinda,' she confessed. 'It's like, for the first time in my career, albeit short, I understand what loss really feels like. How I must have encroached on so many grieving parents and siblings and widows, without a second thought. I didn't feel it so badly with Dad, maybe because of his illness and age, and … and we expected him to go. Warren was snatched away from me. I'm such a bad person.'

Dorinda tutted loudly. 'You're not a bad person, darling. You're one of the most caring and compassionate people I know. Yes, you've faced some difficult stories since working at the paper, but you would never have made anyone feel uncomfortable about their grief.'

She wiped the sleeve of her robe across her nose. 'They're not stories, sis, this is real life. People's sorrow and heartache. But I know what you're trying to get at and … thank you.'

'Now, what have the police told you about Warren?'

'Bloody nothing. It's driving me insane. I thought his body was being released, but now I think someone in Ambleside just told me that to get me off the phone. I rang again this morning. They said the Inspector dealing with the case would get back to me, but I've heard nothing.' Her voice croaked, as the air caught in her throat. 'And to top it off, the local police have reopened Donna's missing case.'

'Oh, well, that's good news, isn't it? They must have a pretty good reason to do so, after all this time. Although, I remember the state you were in after she disappeared … Felicity, this is a lot for you to handle right now. Shall I come and stay with you for a few days? I could help around the house, or just be there when you need a shoulder … or a bottle of wine. At least until you know more about what's going on. And when Warren will be coming home for the funeral … It will help with the grief, sweetie.'

Felicity closed her eyes on the burning tears erupting from them. She could barely speak, overwhelmed by her sister's kindness. Despite being five years older, Dorinda always made an effort to support her; visiting prospectus universities, helping with the move to Uxbridge, and filming graduation day. Their father had passed away ten years ago, and Felicity's memories of him grew fainter with each passing year. Instead, the memory which played vividly in her mind was that of her mother, who, just a few days after her father's funeral, had returned to work and her weekly outing to the bingo hall. Felicity had been in awe of her mother; a woman who pushed all her pain and anguish to one side in order to be a strong role model for her daughters. It was because of this strength of character Felicity had found it difficult to accept the doctor's dementia diagnosis. Watching her beloved mother move into a residential care home, three years earlier, broke her heart. But in true, Irish women style, Dorinda had taken up the protective baton, even throughout her pregnancy.

'Thank you, I appreciate the offer, but I can't accept.'

'Why not?' Dorinda replied quickly.

Felicity sighed. 'Because you have a family and a home of your own to take care of. Besides, who would look after my beautiful niece while you're here, plying me with alcohol and wiping my snots?'

'I'm sure Amelia's father could manage a few nights alone just fine. Plus, we've just hit the beginning of the terrible-twos phase, and even the thought of one night away sounds like paradise at the moment.'

She smiled, picturing her fanatic, neat-freak sister trying to handle Amelia. A brunette mini version of Dorinda, who had no interest in rules and spoke a language only other toddlers could understand.

'Actually, why don't you come and stay with us?' Dorinda interrupted her thoughts. 'It would be so great to have you here. The three of us could do some fun, girlie activities. And William wouldn't mind at all. He'd probably see it as a mini-break for himself.' Her sister laughed.

She cringed. It wasn't that Felicity didn't enjoy William's company; he'd been friendly since the day she'd met him. And she had introduced the pair. But the whirlwind romance, resulting in Dorinda's positive pregnancy test just a few weeks later, bothered her. Felicity was a true traditionalist, and while she'd never be sorry her niece came into their lives, she envisioned a couple owning their own home and saying their vows before starting a family. Her friends had mocked her constantly when she first aired her old-school views, so she stopped telling people. She couldn't be sure why she felt the way she did; her parents had rented their family home and only entered the idea of a young marriage when her mother fell pregnant. Her sister, ever the pessimist, never mentioned marriage, but Felicity knew it was something Dorinda secretly wanted. Except William never proposed. Her thoughts quickly turned to Warren, and the way he'd gone down on bended knee.

'Felicity, love, are you still there?' Dorinda disturbed her once again.

She exhaled heavily. 'I'm here, and this is where I'll be staying. Thank you, it really does mean a lot, knowing you're there for me. But … this is where I need to be. Don't worry. I'll be fine on my own, I promise.'

'I'll always worry about you. You're my little sister. But independence flows through our bodies as powerful as the blood in our veins, so I understand. Keep me updated about Warren, and Donna, won't you?'

'Of course, thank you,' Felicity paused. 'Listen, someone's just knocked, I'll have to go. Speak soon. Love you.'

As Felicity descended the stairs, she realised the noise echoed from the back of the house, rather than the front door, as she'd thought. Her paced slowed, and she bent her head forward, listening for any sound out of place.

The handle squeaked.

The latched clicked.

The back door closed.

Someone is in my house.

There was no access to her garden from the street. She'd tossed her mobile back onto the bed before leaving the room, and despite her brain telling her to run back and call for help, she gravitated towards the kitchen. Every breath felt heavy inside her tight chest. Her feet reluctantly tip-toed onto the next step. She wiped her clammy hands down the dressing gown as she reached the hallway.

The silence was deafening. Barefoot, she crept across the carpeted floor and froze outside the kitchen door. Nothing. She grabbed the bronze statue of entwined lovers from the floating shelf on the wall.

Felicity inhaled deeply and pushed open the door. Stepping forward into the middle of the kitchen, she raised the sculpture high above her head and peered around like a sentry on duty. As she turned and looked behind her, the statue dropped and smashed into pieces. She gasped, the smell suddenly attacking her nostrils. Her hands instinctively flew up, covering her nose and mouth. Silent tears streamed down her face, while she read the shit smeared message on the white kitchen wall: *Tell the truth … or you're next!*

CHAPTER ELEVEN

Delighted to return to the office and find an array of missed calls and messages from officials in the Cumbria Constabulary, Hamilton instructed his team to communicate the intelligence they'd uncovered. While they made detailed notes on the evidence board, he left them and headed for his office.

Despite Inspector Bennett demanding his call be returned immediately, his patience was obviously trying, as Hamilton spied an urgent email flagged red waiting in his inbox. Momentarily distracted, he read Fraser's scribbled message, explaining the pathologist, Amy Sullivan, also needed his attention. The name wasn't familiar, but the anticipation of possibly uncovering information about Warren Speed's post-mortem bubbled inside him. However, he realised the Chief must have been successful in pulling a few strings, so he thought it only fair to address Inspector Bennett first.

He grabbed the phone receiver while glancing over the email. Frowning, he moved in closer to the screen, surprised to read Inspector Bennett had granted permission for the Met to take over Speed's investigation. With its links to London, and their lack of evidence pointing to a possible suspect, he assured Hamilton his team would do their upmost to assist him. Bennett had already liaised with the pathologist, his PSCOs were in the process of collating all the case information, and Hamilton would have everything by the end of the day. He raised an eyebrow, nodding as he read over the final paragraph. He hadn't expected such swift movement from Bennett, and it impressed him. Whether the sarcastic Inspector was happy about it or not, things were rolling in Hamilton's direction. Content that the email explained all he needed, and eager, now more than ever, to get Amy Sullivan on the phone, he punched in the number left for her. He drummed his fingers on the desk while the dialling tone droned his ear. He heard the American twang of the woman's voice immediately, and realised she was the pathologist he'd met at the Lake Windermere crime scene.

'I've been expecting your call. Thanks for getting back to me,' she said.

'The pleasure is all mine. I'm glad Inspector Bennett has given the go-ahead for you to share the post-mortem details with me. Anything you can tell me at this stage would be appreciated.'

'I think I'll be able to tell you quite a bit, Detective. I've received the toxicology report for Mr Speed, and we've discovered something interesting.'

Hamilton frowned. 'I got the impression Inspector Bennett didn't have much evidence to go on.'

Amy groaned, almost a light-heartedly chuckle. 'Some people don't like being told … they don't have time for things they can't understand, or have no control over, shall we say. But I suppose I can only speak for myself when I say what we've found is extremely helpful to the case.'

He imagined he wasn't the first to dislike Inspector Bennett's way of working, and he smiled to himself. He'd enjoy working with this fiery pathologist.

'I'm all ears. Give me what you've got,' Hamilton said and poised his pen to make quick notes.

Amy spent a few minutes explaining that Warren Speed had been injected with a lethal toxin, prior to the twenty-one stabs wounds to his back. Before his death, Speed suffered from botulism, a fatal condition that involves muscle paralysis.

'Wait,' Hamilton interrupted. 'Why does this botulism poison sound so familiar?'

'You and Joe Public would refer to it as Botox.'

'Are you trying to tell me Warren Speed was Botoxed to death?' His chuckle was immediately followed by a wince; had he reacted in the exact same manner as Inspector Bennett? 'Sorry, Amy. Please continue with the details.'

She cleared her throat, and he could imagine her rolling her eyes at his comment. 'The recommended doses of Botox used for cosmetic treatments are too low to cause a systematic disease. However, an injection of unlicensed and highly concentrated botulinum toxin may cause severe botulism.'

'And just explain what that actually is again, please,' Hamilton said, while writing furiously on his notepad.

'Botulism is a rare disease but potentially fatal … and in Mr Speed's case, it was maliciously given via two injections in his neck. It begins with the weakness of the body; he may also have suffered blurred vision and speech problems. There would have been cranial nerve and muscle paralysis, shortly followed by paralysis of the respiratory system.'

Hamilton blew a puff of hot air and lowered his pen, the information swirling around his mind. 'Jesus! I can hardly believe what you're telling me.'

'Inspector Bennett had the same problem. Anyway, botulinum toxin is one of the most potent toxins known,' Amy continued. 'I did of bit of research before I called you because, I won't lie, Botox is not my field of expertise. Plus, you don't see it used as a murder weapon a lot on the shores of Windermere. Now, although the exact lethal dosage can't be quantified, it's estimated that a man of roughly eleven stone would need to be injected with between 0.09 and 0.15 milligrams of the toxin to cause this amount of damage.'

Hamilton hummed slightly. He wanted her to know he was still listening and taking the details seriously – if this was the evidence the toxicology report gave him, he'd take it – but he needed things to form a clear pattern of understanding in his mind.

She must have understood; Amy continued to fire more information. 'Okay, you must have seen images of the small bottles or vials that are regularly used for these types of things in hospitals and clinics, right? That one vial contains 0.5 milligrams of Botox. Your murderer would have only needed to get their hands on a couple of vials, inject it into Mr Speed, and wait for the weakness to take over … which wouldn't have taken long at all.'

'Would he have been aware of his surroundings, or the knife attack?'

Amy sighed. 'It's hard to say for sure. It also depends how long the killer waited after the Botox was injected before the attack, but it's possible he knew. He would have literally been helpless to stop it.'

Hamilton shook his head. 'I'm still trying to get my head around this. People really will use anything at their disposal. So, which of the two was the actual cause of death?'

'It's too close to call. Untreated, the injection overdose would have broken down his muscles and respiratory system – there really was no need for anything else. But the multiple stab wounds meant he lost a lot of blood. I couldn't find anything of significance about those wounds, except the sheer frantic nature of them, and that your killer carried some serious upper body strength.'

'Or was consumed by complete rage,' Hamilton added. 'Was there anything else of interest found at the scene, the footprints, perhaps?'

'There were far too many in the end, Detective. My team took some samples of those nearest to the dock, but in reality, they could have been from the tourists running from the vessel. We're still working on it. A single cigarette butt was found, next to where we found samples of Mr Speed's blood in the soil. It's also being tested, and other examinations are still being performed. But I'm happy to release the body to the family now. If there's anything we find that can assist you, I'll be in touch straight away.'

'Thank you, Amy,' Hamilton said and swapped the receiver into his other hand, rubbing the left, clammy one along his trousers. 'I appreciate the level of detail you've given me.'

They bid each other farewell, and Hamilton sat back in the chair, soaking up the silence. His mind buzzed with unanswered questions, possible scenarios, and potential leads. Astonished at the facts he'd just learnt, he was grateful his wife had never been interested in the Botox hype, especially as so many of her friends had. Granted, the pathologist had explained that, cosmetically, it wasn't lethal, yet the thought of how something injected into people on a daily basis could so easily be used to overpower and kill a man, made him shudder.

* * *

'Are you really so surprised, boss?' Dixon said, after Hamilton relayed the information to the team. 'You can extract poisons from leaves that grow freely in some countries. Did you know if you eat the leaves of a hemlock plant, you're wide awake to any and all pain, but your body is paralysed?'

'You know a lot about this stuff.' Clarke raised his hands and stepped away with a grin.

'Remind us never to accept a dinner invitation at your house,' Rocky chimed in.

Fraser laughed. 'Isn't that what happened to Michelle Pfeiffer in that film … what was it called … Oh, yes, What Lies Beneath?'

'Yes, I've seen that,' Dixon exclaimed. 'It sounds familiar, but I can't remember what was used; I don't think it was hemlock.'

Hamilton crossed his arms over his broad chest. The sound of his tanned loafers slapping against the tiled floor brought their conversation to a sudden halt.

'So, are we saying the killer could be a doctor or a nurse? Or perhaps a dermatologist?' Rocky asked.

'It's possible, I guess.' Hamilton sighed. 'We need to do a bit more digging into Botox and how easily accessible it is to the general public. The killer would have only needed a couple of vials, so the pathologist led me to believe. Find out if it's easy to buy, or would the killer need to work in the vicinity of such establishments in order to swipe what he needed. We now know how Warren Speed died, but nothing leading up to his death, or why he visited Lake Windermere. That's our top priority; I want to know what his movements were in the days before his murder and who he spoke to. Also, let's revisit Felicity Ireland and delve more into her fiancé's life, separate to Donna Moran's disappearance.'

'Before we crack on, gov, let me just quickly bring you up to speed,' Clarke said. 'We managed to pin down Todd Bell at home, but we couldn't track down Holly Walker. Fraser's digging about now to see if she has a work address.'

Hamilton perched on the desk next to his partner. 'Okay, you two hang back with Fraser and dig into the information we need for Warren Speed. Dixon and I will cover Ireland and Walker. What did you get from Todd?'

'Nothing really, boss,' Rocky answered. 'Felt like a waste of time, if I'm honest. He pretty much re-told his original statement.'

He accepted Rocky's honesty, knowing it was exactly that, rather than a complaint. 'Yes, seems to be a recurring theme with this bunch of friends.'

Clarke rubbed a hand over his square jaw line and grunted. 'Ever get the feeling we're looking at the wrong people, and that we should be concentrating more on Donna Moran's whereabouts. I mean, it was *her* name found inside Warren Speed's mouth. Perhaps this group of friends aren't telling us anything different because there is nothing new.'

'But if that's the case, we can't ignore the fact they could all be potential victims,' Dixon added.

Hamilton enjoyed watching his team debate. It was in moments like this they uncovered new leads, or ways of thinking. He also thought it was a great way for them to bond, without it being forced. He got a real insight to their personalities when they were just throwing about their ideas for the investigation.

'I take everything on board,' he said. 'I don't think it will do any harm interviewing all those who had a close connection to Donna Moran and her disappearance. We'll couple that with research we gather on Warren Speed, see if we can ascertain why he was at Lake Windermere, and go from there. Fraser, did you get a chance to speak with Joan Moran?'

She brushed the loose strands of blonde hair over her shoulder and crossed her legs. 'I did, and the news of her daughter's case being re-opened was a huge shock to the woman. She was at work, so I said I'd pop into her later, on my way home, and have a chat with her. She sounded quite shaky on the phone. I think face-to-face would be easier for her to comprehend.'

Hamilton nodded, regretting the way he'd originally allowed Fraser to liaise with the mother. After all, he of all people understood the agony of losing a child; worse for this woman who knew nothing of her daughter's whereabouts.

'Yes, that's definitely a more sensitive approach,' he said. 'Leave here whenever you need to, Fraser. We'll see you first thing in the morning, if we're not back by the time you head off.'

CHAPTER TWELVE

'It's a good thing you phoned ahead to see if Felicity Ireland was still at work,' Hamilton said, as he indicated and manoeuvred onto the North Circular from Western Avenue.

'Yes, it's just a shame her home is double the distance than her place of work is from the station,' Dixon replied and gazed out the window.

He clicked the button on his door, allowing the window to roll down halfway. The cool breeze, as he accelerated to forty miles per hour, was welcoming; the tension in his small Corsa stifling. He'd hoped to have made some connection with the newest member of his team by now, and knew he'd have to bite the bullet sooner rather than later.

The speed dropped as Hamilton took the exit for Harrow and Wembley, and they were soon cruising through Stonebridge. Stopped at a red light, he took in the area and marvelled at the different cuisines available in one row of shops: Italian, Jamaican, Indian, and Chinese. It mirrored the diversity of ethnicities of the people mulling around the street. It was one of the reasons he loved London; no matter what postcode he found himself in, it was always submerged in a richness of cultures.

The iconic Arch of Wembley Stadium dominated the view as they progressed on their journey. Illuminated in a brilliant, white shining light, it was hard to miss. Thankfully, an event hadn't been scheduled for the venue this evening, as it disrupted the traffic and parking considerably. Of course, when he'd visited for a football match a few months previously, he couldn't have cared less, happy to mill along the pavement with other supporters. But when trying to drive even ten minutes down the road, with revellers walking out in front of the cars dismissively, or diversions and road blocks along the path, he could understand the frustrations event days brought the locals.

'Ever attended an event at Wembley?' he asked.

'Yeah, we came to see *Disney on Ice* last Christmas with the … kids. Obviously.' She bit her lip and looked away from him again.

Hamilton sighed, took the next left onto Uphill Drive, and parked on the single yellow line outside Felicity Ireland's home. Once he'd cut the engine and unclipped his seatbelt, he turned to face Dixon.

'I hope you know, you can talk about your kids without feeling guilty,' he said bluntly.

She finally returned his gaze, the richness of her sun-kissed skin highlighted the warmth in her brown eyes. But he couldn't help noticing the sadness in them too, and wondered if there was something more she refused to share with him.

'I just feel like a prat,' she finally blurted. 'My comment earlier was cruel and insensitive, and I should have known better. Your lovely wife was kind enough to share with me what you both suffered … losing a child is just … it's just unthinkable amounts of pain. Then I come to work, wanting to make a good impression with you, but instead, I rock up to the office late, speak without thinking, and end up sounding like a right crank.'

Hamilton laughed at the turn of phrase she used to call herself an idiot. She may look exotic and mysterious, but Dixon couldn't have sounded more like a Londoner than she did in that moment, he thought. He appreciated how nervous she must feel, and knew it was imperative they formed some semblance of a relationship in order to understand each other.

'Listen, everyone's life story has its scars. You've seen mine. They're painful and never-ending, but ultimately, they make us who we are. The demons in my life will haunt me forever, but I wouldn't want anyone to treat me differently because of them. Don't stand on ceremony around me, don't feel like you can't share your experiences with me – the good and the bad. Especially those involving your children. My team are all very important to me, and I want to work closely with each and every one of you. How other people's stories play out sometimes depends on us.'

Dixon nodded and slowly smiled. 'That's a nice way to look at things, boss, and thank you. I'm grateful for the kindness you've shown me.'

'Let's chalk this up as a lesson learnt, and move on.'

'Sounds like a plan. Now, let's get back to business.'

The tension visibly subsided from her shoulders as she mirrored Hamilton's movements, unclipping her seatbelt and exiting the car. The pair walked across the road and headed for a large town house. A perfectly tended to front garden welcomed them. Surrounded with charming trimmed hedges, it offered privacy to the downstairs windows from the busy street. A small water fountain, adorned with colourful flowers, and a jet-washed path led to a polished black door. They waited a few minutes, almost prepared to give-up, when Felicity finally answered wearing yellow marigolds and a deep flush to her cheeks.

'Miss Ireland, we would like to have another chat with you please,' Hamilton explained.

'I'm sorry, no … now is not a good time,' Felicity replied and pulled the rubber gloves from her hands.

'I promise we won't take too much of your time. But it's imperative we discuss Warren Speed with you.'

Worried the woman would slam the door in their face, Hamilton took a step closer. It was then he noticed the sweat beads glistening on her forehead and heard the sharp panting of her breath. He peered over her shoulder into the house, but could see, or hear nothing of interest.

'Is everything okay, Miss Ireland?' Hamilton asked. 'You look a little flustered.'

'Yes,' she replied quickly. 'I'm fine, just … keeping busy. Come in.' She pulled the door open further and stepped back into the large hallway.

'Thank you,' he said and followed Felicity inside.

Suddenly, she rushed in and pulled a door closed. 'I'm painting the kitchen at the moment, you know, keeping my hands busy, like I said. We can talk through here.'

Once they were all settled in the grand, yet homely, living room, Hamilton explained the progress of Warren's investigation and his team's involvement.

'He was drugged, with Botox? What … I don't understand,' Felicity explained. 'I didn't even know that was possible. I've heard nothing like it before.'

Hamilton nodded. 'I appreciate this is a lot of information to digest at once. Further tests are still to be conducted, and we'll keep you informed. In the meantime, we'd like to get a better understanding of your fiancé's life.'

Felicity sighed, her watering eyes focused on the floor. 'What do you want to know?'

'We need to know why Warren travelled to Ambleside, what his plans were, and if he was alone.'

'I don't know,' Felicity replied and looked at Hamilton; her face reddened, not flushed any longer, but stained with a mixture of old and fresh tears.

He frowned. 'Were you in the habit of going on weekends away without telling each other the details?'

'Detective, we're both very busy … *were* very busy people. Our jobs are demanding and not your normal nine-to-five. For Warren, also being in the public eye, he often had to dart off to promotional events and such like. He said he'd be back Sunday, and that was all I knew.'

'So, you did know he was travelling somewhere?'

Felicity exhaled loudly through her nose. 'Yes. He sent me a text on Saturday morning, to let me know he'd be away for the night. He was hoping to secure a TV interview, but that was all the information he gave me, I didn't know where he was going. I was shocked to find out it was Ambleside. He hasn't returned there since …'

'Since your friend, Donna, went missing.' Hamilton finished her sentence. 'Would anyone else have been privy to Warren's travel arrangements?'

'His personal assistant, Claire Newcomb, probably would have arranged the tickets for him. I haven't managed to talk to her yet though. I'm in the dark as much as you, Detective. When will I be able to see Warren ... Oh God! I don't know if I can see him. Was he badly beaten? Does he still look like the Warren I know?'

Felicity allowed the tears to gush down her cheeks, as she cupped her hands over her face.

Hamilton moved forward to the edge of the beige two-seater sofa and spoke softly to her. 'Warren's body will be released shortly, and you can begin organising the funeral. I'm sure we can arrange for you to see him first, if that's what you choose. It's a very natural human need to see the things that upset us the most. Once it's real in your mind, it makes it easier to mourn and move on.'

She inhaled deeply, brushing the wet streams away with the back of her hand and nodded in agreement. 'Thank you.'

'Could we have Claire Newcomb's details, please?' Dixon asked. 'If she conducted Warren's travel arrangements, we need to speak to her immediately.'

'She didn't just arrange them. Claire Newcomb was also with Warren,' Hamilton said.

Felicity gasped. 'What? How do you know that?'

Hamilton took a few moments to explain to both women his involvement with discovering Warren's body, and his brief chat with Claire afterwards.

'Well, maybe she went with him on these things,' Felicity said. 'As his assistant, I guess that makes sense.'

Hamilton watched the creases in her forehead deepen, her eyes focusing on nothing in particular, as though her mind ticked in overdrive. He also realised they would not receive any substantial information from Felicity; when it came to Warren's life, she obviously wasn't the woman in the know.

'I didn't know Claire was with him,' she added, as an afterthought. 'But then, I didn't even know he'd travelled to Lake Windermere. He never wanted to return, not after what happened to Donna,' Felicity repeated herself.

Dixon returned the notebook to her pocket, evidently on the same wavelength as Hamilton. 'Well, something enticed him there.'

Hamilton decided to leave Felicity with that thought, hoping it would spark a memory, or something of use from her. Met with silence, he clenched his fists as they made their way back out onto the street and across to his car.

'What's eating you, boss?' Dixon asked.

'I'm frustrated,' he grumbled. 'We barely know our victim, except he was brutally tortured and secretly visiting Ambleside. We have no suspects, the syringe and knife used to kill him haven't been recovered, and it would take us over four hours on a good day to revisit the crime scene.'

'What about the rope used to tie Speed to the gate?'

'Nothing of interest came back from that, though the team in Ambleside are carrying out more tests. Plus, an item like that could have been purchased from pretty much any shop in town.'

'Are things ever simple when it comes to murder?'

He smiled gingerly and hitched up his shoulder. 'No, I guess you're right. Look, let's call it a day and start fresh tomorrow. Claire Newcomb will be our top priority, and we'll go from there. Can I give you a lift?'

'No, thanks.' Dixon smiled. 'I left Warren, which is actually my husband's name too, with the car today and caught the tube into work. We're only about ten minutes from Wembley Park Station. I can catch a direct link from there.'

'If you're sure?'

'Yeah, I like a good walk sometimes. Blows the cobwebs away, as my Mum used to say, and gives me some much-needed, peaceful thinking time. Who knows what kind of ideas I'll have tomorrow. And I promise I won't be late again.'

It was Hamilton's turn to smile as she waved goodbye, and he climbed into the car. He felt pleased some progress had been made with Dixon; she seemed friendly and professional, and that worked for him. He began the half hour drive back into London, hoping he wouldn't be held up by too much traffic. The desire to get home, put his feet up and chill out overwhelmed him.

Forty minutes later, he eased into his drive and turned off the ignition. Since the night his daughter had taken her own life, Hamilton no longer sat in the car long after he parked, basking in the quietness of his own company. He wanted to be inside his family home, soaking up all the love and familiarity it contained; despite it now only being himself and Elizabeth.

As he slammed the car door shut, Hamilton froze. With no breeze in the late August evening, the rustling of leaves was out of place. He remained motionless, sensitive to every noise around him.

The twig snapping underfoot.

The distinctive panting.

The crunch of shrubbery as a figure emerged from the bushes.

Hamilton spun, just in time to see a large, hooded figure dash from his front garden into the quiet cul-de-sac. The shock took him by surprise, and he faltered for a few moments before giving chase. A silhouette turned left onto the main road, as Hamilton sprinted down the street, humid night air attacking his dry mouth. He came to a stop, bending over and resting his hands on his knees while scanning the main road. Pedestrians strolled along the pavement, cars halted at the red light and people crowded at the nearest bus stop. He couldn't make out where the mystery man had gone.

Turning around to walk home, Elizabeth's face flashed in his mind. The breath caught in this throat. He wildly ran, feet stomping hard against the paving slabs, his thighs as heavy as cement slowed him down. He fell onto the front door, the keys slipping through his sweaty hands. Welcomed by complete silence, the fear shook his entire body while he screamed Elizabeth's name.

Frantically, he opened doors. The living room and kitchen empty. The stillness created a blind mist fogging his eyes.

'Denis, what in heaven's name is wrong?'

He whirled three-hundred and sixty degrees in the hallway to find Elizabeth standing half-way down the stairs in her towelling dressing-gown. The confusion etched on her face clarified nothing out of the ordinary had happened in his house, and he exhaled deeply. He marched towards her, his head dropped onto her stomach as he wrapped his arms around her and drank in her scent. Towering above him from a few steps up, she hushed and hugged him tightly in return.

'I'm sorry. I overacted,' he finally said and pulled away from her.

She walked down to his level. 'You were screaming like a mad man. What happened?'

Hamilton described the events of the past few minutes, which already seemed like hours to him, and how he thought someone had attacked her.

'Jesus, you work for the Met, Denis. Surely you're used to chasing the bad guys?' she said, with a giggle.

He lightly placed a hand on either side of her face. 'I'm not usually running from my own house. And where you're concerned, I'll always worry. If someone was in this house … I don't know what I'd do without you,' he said affectionately.

'Don't be daft. You've ensured this house is like Fort Knox. No-one could get in here without our say so.' She smiled, walked over to the front door, and keyed in the alarm system code. 'There, everything is fine. You never leave things at work, and despite our break away, you're always assuming the worse. You probably imagined seeing someone out there, or it was just kids messing about.'

For a few minutes, he felt foolish. But the more he replayed what had happened since parking on the drive, the more he was certain. He nodded, agreeing with his wife to keep her from joining his anxious mood.

With dinner already prepared, and keeping warm in the oven, Elizabeth suggested they eat in the living room. A comedy film on Netflix was exactly the distraction he needed, she'd said. Cuddling on the sofa, engrossed in a mindless movie each evening, was sometimes exactly what got Hamilton through a difficult day. Occasionally, Clarke would tease him, quipping that he and his wife were old before their time and should live more. He played along with the banter, knowing what he had was actually the thing most men secretly wanted; they were just too afraid to admit it. Yet tonight, he couldn't be further from the enjoyment of a relaxing evening at home.

After they'd eaten, Hamilton drummed his index finger on his closed lips. The television became background noise as he stared through the forty-five-inch set. Later, with Elizabeth ready for bed, he urged her on, explaining he needed to secure downstairs. He lingered in the kitchen for a moment, his mind still racing, and unlocked the back door. Stepping out into the garden, he waited, but nothing came. No security light detected his movement. He listened to the twilight sounds. A light wind whispered in the trees. A distant car engine. A squawk from a nocturnal creature.

Hamilton returned to the kitchen, locked the door, and pulled out a chair at the dining table. Knowing he'd changed the security lights the week before, he thought the chance of another broken bulb so soon too coincidental. Convinced he, his wife, or his house were being watched, he sat firm in his position for the rest of the night, waiting for an attack to come.

CHAPTER THIRTEEN

Fraser watched silently as the woman paced the living room. Just forty-three, the records had indicated, yet Joan Moran's back hunched over, as if too heavy for her slim, frail body to carry. The weight of the world looked like it literally sat on her shoulders, and every step she took pained her to do so. A natural beauty shone through, despite the pale face, sunken skin, and bloodshot eyes; Fraser wondered if the woman had cried every day for past two years.

The faded blue denim of Joan's jeans could easily be attributed to the furious rubbing of her hands, up and down her thighs, over and over again. Her thoughts elsewhere, the woman had mumbled incoherently since Fraser had explained the re-opening of her daughter's case.

The twenty-four-hour BBC news channel played, muted, from the television. Occasionally, Joan's eyes wandered over to read the breaking news, before the marching resumed. The crammed room gave the impression that a busy workaholic used it; a laptop, radio, piles of newspapers, hundreds of missing persons' posters, maps and handwritten notes. It resembled the incident room, on a much smaller scale.

Fraser caught the woman fiddling with a solid gold wedding band on her left hand and frowned. All the information she'd obtained from the Missing Person's database had identified this woman as a single mother. While it was possible Joan had married since Donna's disappearance, she found it highly unlikely.

'Is there someone I can call for you, Joan? Your husband, perhaps?'

'Got a direct line with the devil, have you? He's dead. Five years before Donna left for Brunel, her father stepped out in front of train. I became a widower and single parent overnight. I don't know why I've never taken this thing off,' she said, signalling to the ring. 'There's no redemption for suicide, you know? It's the biggest sin.'

At that moment, Fraser noticed the bible on the small side-table by the armchair opposite her. The cracked spine, various creases, and tatty pages turned down were clearly evident.

'Are you a religious family?' Fraser asked.

Joan shook her head. 'I wasn't … not until last year. The local church is a pillar of strength, and the people help me distribute leaflets and photographs of Donna.'

'How was your daughter, after her father died? I mean, did she bottle-up her feelings? Perhaps it could explain why she ran away?'

Joan finally took a seat in the armchair and sighed. 'They weren't very close … they just didn't get each other. Donna is very logical and academic, and likes to get things done. Keith … the total opposite. After the redundancy, everything just snowballed downhill for him. Depression took hold of him.' She wiped a single tear away and crossed her arms. 'Donna and I … we were there for each other, but neither of us fell apart.'

Fraser nodded, sensing it caused the woman pain, but the need to delve further into Donna's disappearance urged her on. 'Do you think you could tell me, from your own perspective, about Donna's weekend away, and the events that followed it?'

Joan sprung from her seat, pacing again, and talking at full speed. 'My daughter did not run away. She was happy, and looking forward to securing a job now she'd graduated with flying colours. I never received a text or a phone call to say she was coming back to London … you see, it just doesn't make sense.'

'But the Cumbria Constabulary were satisfied Donna had left Ambleside –'

'Don't give me that!' Joan interrupted, perched on the edge of the armchair and wagged her index finger in the air. 'Those country coppers couldn't give a shit about a girl from London who didn't find her way home.'

'I've read the files, Joan. The inspector in charge examined the CCTV footage of Ambleside station and identified Donna catching the train towards London on Sunday morning.'

Joan blew her lips together, like a child blowing a raspberry. 'Ha! Please. It was a grainy clip, ten seconds, if that, of the back of a blonde girl with a backpack like Donna's. It could have been anyone, for crying out loud. And what about the coppers here? As much use as a flaming chocolate teapot.' The woman's tempo increased. 'They wouldn't check the CCTV at Waterloo or Kings Cross to see if that's where Donna got off the train.'

'That could have taken days. She didn't use the pre-ordered train ticket with her friends, and there was no way of the Constabulary finding out which ticket she'd purchased from the machine at the station before heading off to London … if that was indeed her direction of travel.'

'They didn't make an appeal on *Crimewatch*, or the news, like I've seen for so many other kids.'

'Donna was twenty-one.'

'There wasn't even an article in the national papers.'

'These cases are very difficult.' Fraser waited, but Joan had run out of steam and wasn't interrupting anymore. 'We have to take into account Donna's age and no danger of foul play. She was with her friends …'

'Exactly! Why would she just leave Warren and Holly? She loved them. She would have told them why, given them a reason … I know she would have.'

Fraser asked Joan about Donna and Warren's relationship, not wanting to give too much evidence away. The woman reaffirmed the pair had indulged in a bit of fun, but according to her daughter, it had been nothing serious.

'Donna has an amazing spirit. Everyone is drawn to her,' Joan said, relaxing slightly in the chair and staring at a spot over Fraser's head. 'She wants to please everyone. She's the listener, the joker, the confidante, the leader, or … whatever role you need for her to be. Donna bends herself to suit her friends. I never appreciated it before; it was just her way. But I understand now that those types of people are actually stronger than any of us. They take everything on board, selflessly readjust themselves, and become who their friends need. Over the years, she did that for me, especially when I wasn't the strongest of mothers. I took it for granted.'

Joan dragged her concentration back to the present and met Fraser's gaze for a few seconds. The woman shook her head and moved to the edge of the chair, before continuing. 'Anyway, it was their university years. Donna and Warren were a bit of fun; my girl didn't need a man tying her down. Although, I think that Felicity had a problem with it more than anyone else. Of all Donna's friends, I liked her the least … I never trusted her. There was something about her that didn't feel real. Mothers can sense these things.'

Joan continued to bash Felicity Ireland's character for a few more minutes, while Fraser made mental notes. She didn't want to disturb the women while she was being so forthcoming about the friends they were investigating. Suddenly, Joan stopped talking and look directly at Fraser. The woman's brown eyes grew black, the heavy bags under them turned a deeper shade of purple.

'You think Donna's disappearance is connected to Warren's death, don't you?'

Despite Hamilton's warning of not giving away too much information, Fraser's heart pulled when she looked at the desperate woman in front of her.

'Please, Detective … I have to know.'

Fraser inhaled deeply. 'Yes. Donna's case has been reopened because we feel there could be a link with Warren Speed's murder.'

Joan slid her hands between her thighs and squeezed tightly. 'Thank you.'

A stream of tears ran from the woman's eyes, and Fraser knew it best she left now, before she lost all professionalism and disclosed every piece of evidence they'd uncovered so far.

'That's all I can tell you right now … it's all I know. But I promise the moment information can be shared, you'll be informed. I'll leave you my card, in case you think of anything, or if Donna does get in touch.'

The woman's head sprung up. 'You think my baby is still alive?'

Fraser's stomach lurched. Regardless of age, her mother would also refer to her as "my baby." Her chest tightened as she attempted to answer Joan's question. Luckily, there was no need; the woman had resumed to her own thoughts.

'We must have faith, Detective. I know, deep in my soul, something awful has happened to Donna. There is no explanation for why she wouldn't get in contact with me. But I have to hope God is watching over her, and that he'll guide her back to me.'

With that, the woman picked up her bible and disappeared into a trance. Fraser lightly squeezed Joan's shoulder as she left the room, and the deathly quiet house.

* * *

Rocky walked into the kitchen and gasped at the scene greeting him. Fraser sat shivering, despite the unnecessary heat pumping from the radiators, at the round dining table. Wrapped in a star motif dressing gown, Fraser's blonde locks were scraped away from her face with a clip. Her glare remained fixed on the large box in front of her, even as he stepped further inside the room. Although Rocky felt the urge to rush to her side and console her, he lingered back, waiting for an explanation. Fraser usually exuded such control and confidence at work, yet now, she appeared more like a victim than his colleague.

'The door was left ajar,' he said, while looking around the small room for any sign of foul play.

'I heard your car pull up. I opened it as I came downstairs,' Fraser replied, her voice barely a whisper.

He pulled out the only other available chair and perched next to her. 'I was just on my way to the office when you called this morning.'

She nodded, but her attention remained on the box. 'I'm sorry. I didn't really know what to do. Stupid really, considering what I do for a living. I contemplated phoning Clarke, but I thought he'd just laugh at me.'

'Kerry, it's okay, I won't laugh. You can tell me whatever you need to.' He followed her eyes to the unidentified object. 'Can I open the box?'

Fraser nodded, covered her face with her hand and turned away. Rocky rubbed his palms along his thighs, wiping the sweat onto his starched, black trousers. He slowly lifted the rectangular, white box and froze. A bouquet of lilies, the petals and stems brown and lifeless, riddled with worms and insects. Rocky yelped, flipping the lid back on the box after a beetle scurried along the edge of the decaying wreath.

'Fuck sake,' he yelled, forgetting all professionalism. 'What's all this about?'

She turned her body to him, but continued staring at the white tiled floor. 'I found them on my front step this morning. They have to be from Johnny … he knows lilies are my favourite.'

Before Rocky could enquire who Johnny was, he stopped himself. Still a stranger, having only worked together for a few weeks, he wondered if Fraser would truly feel comfortable opening up to him. He studied her every move; the way she fidgeted with the wisps of hair around her face, then clasping her hands together and rolling one thumb around the other. He heard the deep sigh, before her watery eyes met his.

'Johnny is … was … my best friend. And, no, nothing more than that, before you ask. Sometimes a man and woman *can* just be friends,' Fraser blurted. 'One of the last cases I worked on, a young girl lost her friend to drugs, and I could totally empathise with her. Except my friend didn't die … nevertheless, I still lost him. Over the years of his addiction, he hurt me in ways I don't think anyone else could. Lied to and stole from me, used the secrets we shared to manipulate me and get what he wanted. I couldn't watch it anymore. I couldn't be a part of what he was doing to himself. So, I moved to Central London … no, not a million miles away from my home town in Kent, but it's very easy to get lost in London, and that's what I wanted. I started a new life for myself.'

'What makes you think these are from Johnny then?' Rocky asked, after she'd remained silent for a few moments.

She wiped the mix of tears and snot that had silently mingled together. 'After I left, I kept in touch with a mutual friend. Occasionally, I'd get in touch with her, for an update on Johnny. Last year, she told me he'd finally gone into rehab and was doing really well. About six months ago, she asked if I'd meet with him, said he needed my forgiveness to move on. I thought about it, but I couldn't go back to that. I gave him chance after chance before and always ended up getting hurt. I'm happy here with my job. I couldn't jeopardise that.'

'So, you didn't meet up with him.'

'No,' she said and gazed back at the floor. 'I wrote our friend a letter, asking her to pass it onto Johnny. I asked him never to get in touch with me again, hoping it would give us both some closure.'

Rocky nodded towards the flower box. 'I'm assuming he took it the wrong way.'

'Exactly. Full of destruction and spitefulness … that's the Johnny I remember. Unfortunately.'

'Look, Kerry, I think we should tell the boss about this.'

She leapt up from the chair. 'No, we can't. I'll look weak and vulnerable.'

'Of course you won't. But you said it was on your front step, and there's no delivery notice with them, which means they were hand delivered. Johnny knows where you live.'

A darkness descended over Fraser's face, but she quickly shook it away and walked around the table. 'I'm sure this is just an answer to my letter, and nothing more will come of it.'

Rocky followed suit, standing to face Fraser. 'I understand your reservations, but I don't think it'll harm us to tell him –'

'Please, Rocky, there's no need,' she interrupted him, her professional persona restored. 'I'm sorry, I never should have called you. What I should have done was thrown that awful box in the bin, had a shower, and got myself into work.'

'Hey, it's okay. Despite everything, it would have been a shock.' Rocky smiled and stepped forward with his arms outstretched.

Fraser backed away. 'Please don't be nice to me, Rocky. I don't want to fall apart. I shouldn't have got all emotional and dragged you into this. It's my mess.'

He lowered his hands, but stepped closer again. 'Would you bloody stop saying sorry,' he replied jovially. 'We've all got baggage we'd prefer not to have.'

She busied herself, swiping a glass from the cupboard and filling it with water. Rocky couldn't help but notice how her hand shook while she held it under the tap.

'Rocky, I just need you to give the boss an update from me, about Mrs Moran. If that's okay?'

'No problem, whatever you need me to do.' He wanted to be sterner, not care about what she'd just divulged with him, which was obviously what she wanted too. But the pain etched on Fraser's face was too much to ignore. 'You don't have to come into work today. I can cover for you.'

'Don't be daft. Of course I'll be at work,' she quickly replied. 'I have a lead to chase up first, about the Botox, but I should be in by lunchtime. Actually, I don't think I told Hamilton and the team. Could you?'

'Like I said, no problem.' Rocky grabbed the box from the middle of the table and walked out of the kitchen. After opening the front door, he stopped, peered over his shoulder, and heard the faint sound of sobs. He wanted to be a trustworthy friend and colleague, but his inner self screamed this was something Hamilton should be told about. He'd battle with himself the entire journey into the office.

'See you in a few hours,' he yelled and pulled the door shut after no reply came.

CHAPTER FOURTEEN

Felicity waited in the doorway as her friends walked through to her kitchen. A whistle echoed from Todd's lips, while Holly's eyes widened and she stood, stunned and silent, for a few moments. Their questions and theories soon attacked Felicity in quick succession, and the pain coursed from the top of her skull to the base of her neck like a blaze of fire. Drained, she walked into the living room and slumped into the armchair, knowing the pair would soon follow suit.

'Have you called the police?' Holly asked, and took a seat on the sofa.

Todd perched next to the redhead and leaned forward, his arms resting on his thighs and his hands clasped together. Felicity could feel both sets of watchful eyes drilling into her, and she lowered her chin to her chest and studied the floor.

'No, what's the point?'

'There's every point,' Holly exclaimed. 'Warren's just been murdered, and someone's broken into your home telling you you're next. Why haven't you called them already?'

'Because she knows who it is.' Todd's deep voice cut through the air, and Felicity lifted her head. 'It's Donna, isn't it?'

The tears welled beneath her lashes, threatening to erupt. Despite having experiencing every emotion possible with the two friends sitting in front of her, she didn't feel comfortable to openly weep. The past two years had changed their relationship dramatically, and she was afraid they'd get up and leave her; the last thing Felicity wanted was to be alone.

'We need to get Calvin here,' Todd continued.

'I asked you all to come around in the group message. He read it, but didn't reply.'

'Probably because you didn't give us the heads up about this. He has a right to know.'

Holly threw her arms in the air. 'Know what?'

'Are you stupid, woman?' Todd said. 'Don't you see what's going on here? Donna's back, and she wants revenge for what happened at Lake Windermere. First Warren, now Felicity … any one of us could be next.'

Felicity watched the argument between her two friends like a tennis volley. Although surprised by Todd's quick conclusion, she couldn't help but agree with him; Warren's body had been found at the exact spot they'd last seen Donna, and the police re-opening the missing person's file caused the panic, which had simmered silently for years, to boil to the surface. Now, Todd voiced what she'd been too afraid to say.

'You're having a fucking laugh,' Holly exclaimed, and stood up. 'Donna wouldn't do this … she couldn't kill Warren. One of her best friends, and he was more than just a friend to her.' She folded her arms and looked at Felicity briefly. 'Sorry … but you know what I mean. You're both overreacting. I can't believe Donna would do this.'

'*Tell the truth, or you're next*. That's what it says on the wall.' Todd pointed in the direction of the kitchen. 'What else could that mean? It's a bloody warning for all of us to come clean about Lake Windermere.'

'Why would Donna wait two years?' Holly fired back. 'Our friend, who studied creative writing, suddenly turned into Jason Bourne and has been hiding out all this time, planning her revenge. Really, that's what you believe?'

Todd rose from the sofa and pointed at Holly. 'Yes, that's what I fucking think,' he said through gritted teeth. 'And if you don't get your head out of la-la land soon, we'll all be in trouble.'

Felicity frowned. 'What do you mean?'

He stood back. 'We're going to need to work together, to find Donna. There's no way we're going to the police, not now, after all this time. Once you change your story, they never believe a word you say. We have to stop her from hurting any of us.'

'This is ridiculous,' Holly moaned, but sat back on the sofa. 'It just all seems … implausible.'

'Look at the facts, Hols, at everything that's happened in the past few weeks. Donna's anniversary … I mean, she couldn't be giving us a bigger clue.'

Felicity nodded. 'Perhaps you're right. But what should we do? I've always looked for Donna and found nothing.'

Holly stared at her. 'Seriously? You continued looking?'

She shrugged, looking down and fumbling with her fingers. 'Not actively on the streets, or anything, but I always ask around and sometimes show her photograph. I needed to make things right. I needed to stop hating myself.'

'I don't know what we'll do, exactly,' Todd interrupted her thoughts. 'But we need Calvin here too; it's not right to do this without him.'

'I've got the car out front. I'll drive to his work and see if he's there,' Holly said and snatched her bag from the floor.

After the front door slammed shut, an unbearable silence filled the house. It drilled into Felicity's ears, a static buzzing noise overtook her thoughts, and she clamped her hands over the side of her head.

'Hey, hey, hey, it's okay,' Todd said and knelt down in front of her. He wrapped his large hands around her shoulders, his hot breath invading her personal space. 'We'll sort all of this out together, just like we used to.'

Felicity sniffed deeply. 'But it's nothing like it used to be. There were six of us then. We had the strongest friendship I'd ever known. We were dragged apart by fear, and we've been thrown back together by murder.'

He rubbed his hands slowly up and down her arms, and her stomach clenched. Like trying to start a camp fire, Todd continued rubbing, and Felicity felt the spark of emotion ignite from deep within her body. She didn't want him to touch her, but she couldn't stop it.

'Listen, Flick, everything happens for a reason. You know I've always been a big believer in that … I've had to be, what with all the shit balls life's thrown at me. After we'd returned from Lake Windermere, things weren't how I wanted them to be, but I had to go with it. We've all just got to ride this rollercoaster of life. But, you need to know, I never stopped thinking about you and the amazing woman you are. You'll always be my best friend.'

Todd ceased his stroking motion and pulled Felicity closer. Heat emerged from her T-shirt, and slid up her neck until her face burned. His warm hands glided onto her back, drawing her into him until she felt dizzy. Their lips touched, softly at first, but passion soon took over, and she could feel Todd's hunger for her. As she allowed his tongue to slip into her mouth, Warren's face filled her mind. Felicity pushed Todd away and jumped up, marching across the room, away from him.

'You have to leave,' she demanded.

He walked towards her. 'Babe, please.'

'I am not your babe! How dare you? You say I'm your best friend, that Warren was too, and then you pull something like this, when you know I'm vulnerable.' She stepped to the side and pointed towards the door. 'I said get out.'

Todd chuckled. 'Now who's overreacting. Come on, let's just forget this happened and move on with –'

'I was wrong to call you here. I don't need you. I haven't needed any of you for two years. I'll sure as hell manage without you now. Leave.'

His smile slipped, and he shook his head as he left the room. Felicity looked away when he stopped in the doorway. She wanted him to understand her message loud and clear: she needed no one.

CHAPTER FIFTEEN

Hamilton stormed into the incident room and slung his jacket over the desk at the back of the office. After updating DCI Allen on the current position of their case, he'd received a bollocking for the lack of progress made. His superior made it quite clear favours had been called upon to have Warren Speed's murder case seamlessly passed from the Cumbria Constabulary to London's MIT, due to Hamilton's imploring.

He sighed as he slumped into the swivel chair nearest the white board and stared at the evidence attached. While he hated being reprimanded, he understood why Allen had been forthcoming with the threats of taking this case from his team. They had nothing of substance to pull them in a viable direction to uncover the clues they needed. Hamilton punched his thigh.

'What's up with you, gov?' Clarke interrupted from behind him.

He turned to face him. 'Well, let's see,' Hamilton replied and counted his fingers as he spoke. 'I hardly got any sleep last night. DCI Allen is on the warpath. We have no flipping suspects. Need I go on?'

Clarke raised his eyebrows. 'I get the picture. But you're really giving us way too much information about the bedroom antics, gov.'

Hamilton's partner returned to his desk with a wink and a cheeky grin. He ignored it, his thoughts drifting to the events of last night. Massaging his crocked neck, Hamilton still needed to discover why the security lights surrounding his home hadn't worked. Instead, he quickly sent Elizabeth a text message, suggesting she stay the night at her mother's, blaming the workload of his current case. Dropping his mobile back into his trouser pocket, he looked up to find Fraser entering the office.

'Ah, nice of you to join us,' he announced, and stood up.

Fraser stopped short and fumbled with the strap of her bag. 'I thought Rocky would have informed you …'

He folded his arms but smiled. 'He did, Fraser, relax. I have an appointment with a witness in an hour. Could you update us quickly?'

She nodded, moving swiftly around the office and grabbing notes from her bag. The rest of the team stopped what they were doing to listen.

'Right, I spoke to a friend of mine who works on Harley Street, and he made it clear that the general public shouldn't be able to readily buy Botox.'

'I feel a "but" coming,' Dixon said.

Fraser cocked her head. 'Well, you'd be right. So, if you search Botox on the internet, you'll find outlets that sell it. However, they will only deliver the product to doctors, dentists, and pharmacies working within licenced establishments. My source backed this up, but she also explained there are some dodgy websites, mainly in the US, that will ship Botox here for people to inject themselves.'

'Or unsuspecting victims,' Rocky added.

'Exactly,' Hamilton agreed. 'I could be wrong, but I'm inclined to think our murderer wouldn't order from the States. It could take weeks.'

'If the killer did in fact lure Warren Speed to Ambleside, time could have been on their side. So, illegally buying the Botox online may have worked.'

Hamilton rubbed his thumb and forefinger back and forth across his lips, mulling everything over. 'It's Claire Newcomb I'm meeting shortly, so maybe she can help us identify exactly why Speed visited the Lakes. But I think we need to delve into his group of friends.'

'There's nothing pointing to them as being involved,' Dixon argued.

'No, but they're all we have right now. If it leads to nothing else, it will discount them as suspects.'

'What do you want us to do then, boss?' Dixon asked.

Hamilton was pleased with her reaction to his challenge; he hadn't agreed with her theory, but she'd taken it professionally. He was learning more about her, and his team in general. Due to the fact Rocky had covered for Fraser earlier that morning, he saw trust forming between them. He'd sussed there was more to what the recruit told him, but, for now, he played along.

'Clarke and I will head out to Claire Newcomb's home address in Hammersmith. Meanwhile, I want the three of you to gather every piece of information on the four friends, namely if any of them have links to the establishments where Botox is readily accessible. Have they ever worked in these places, do their families or partners? If we haven't already, I want a list of subjects they studied at Brunel University. Plus, see if you can ascertain if they were involved in anything suspicious during their time there … apart from Donna Moran's disappearance, of course. By the end of the day, I want a clear understanding in my mind if they're suspects, or potential victims.'

* * *

Hamilton cruised along The Mall towards St. James's Park, and smiled to himself as he thought of his daughter. Growing up, it had been one of Maggie's favourite places to visit on the weekend. Together, they'd walk below the picturesque views of the Shard and the London Eye, standing tall above the glorious greenery and the park's lake, with its two islands: West Island and Duck Island. Maggie had always made a bee-line for the latter island, prepared to spend hours watching the ducks, geese, and pelicans, and feeling a million miles away from the concrete city just yards behind them. As much as he'd enjoyed it, he never really appreciated the time he had with her, and that regret would haunt him forever. Now, he would watch significant events, such as the Virgin London Marathon and Trooping the Colour, take place in that very park and reminisce about his daughter.

Turning right onto Constitution Hill, the monumental Buckingham Palace completely dominated his view. With its gold tipped, iron gates, more windows than he could count, and the British flag flying high at the top of the building, it demanded the attention of passers-by. He wondered how it would feel to be royalty for a day. Not for the wealth and status, but for the protection those grounds offered. Situated in the middle of London, the Royal family may know of the harrowing tragedies and worldly disasters, but what about the crimes happening right outside their front door, Hamilton thought. The life-changing impact of a child missing, a friend murdered, or a mother raped.

'Penny for them?' Clarke dragged him away from his thoughts.

'Ah, just the case.'

His partner groaned. 'Yeah, it's a frustrating one, boss. So, what do we know about this Claire Newcomb?'

'Not much, at present,' Hamilton said and continued to explain how he'd met Newcomb at the crime scene.

In his eyes, Claire was the main witness in the Speed case, and therefore, he couldn't understand why Inspector Bennett and his team had no evidence log of questioning her. If they had at all.

Outside the apartment, Hamilton hammered on the door, while simultaneously pressing the bell marked 1B. His irritation grew as it became apparent there was no one home. He stood back and glanced up at the top window of the white stone detached building. Squinting in the sunlight, he couldn't be sure if the curtain twitched, or if he'd imagined it. Suddenly, the front door flew open.

'I'm Detective Inspector Hamilton, and this is Detective Sergeant Clarke of the Metropolitan Police,' he said and stepped towards the balding man in his late forties. 'I'm looking for Claire Newcomb.'

'I'm Mr Nelson, Detective. I live in 1A, but I could hear all the banging on our communal front door.'

'Sorry to have disturbed you, sir. When's the last time you saw your neighbour?'

The man pushed his dark-rimmed glasses further up his nose and hummed. 'A few days ago, I think. She said she was going away for the weekend, and I haven't seen her since. Mind you, I've read the awful news in the papers about her boss. She must be distraught.'

'What makes you say that?' Clarke intervened.

Mr Nelson crossed his hands and arms in front of him, adopting the stance of an at-ease solider. 'Well, wouldn't you be, Sergeant?'

Hamilton cleared his throat. 'Do you know where Miss Newcomb might have gone? If she has any family near-by, or friends, perhaps?'

Again, the man readjusted his glasses. 'No, I'm sorry, I don't know much about the girl. I mean, she's friendly enough, but she's always come across as a workaholic, not really one to stop for general chit-chat.'

Hamilton nodded, understanding the lack of interaction most neighbours indulged in these days. 'Is that your blue Ford parked outside?'

'Yes, it is. Claire drives a white Mini, if that's why you're asking.'

He grinned. 'Thank you for your time, Mr Nelson, and sorry again for disturbing you. Here's my card. Please do give me a call if Miss Newcomb comes home.'

Hamilton and Clarke turned away, but stopped when the man called out.

'Is Claire in a lot of trouble?'

'We don't know if she's in *any* trouble at all, Mr Nelson. But it is imperative we speak to her regarding her boss's murder investigation.'

'Of course. I'll call you the moment she arrives,' the man replied and shut the front door.

The pair walked out of the front garden and down the street to where Hamilton had parked the car. They both stopped, and Clarke leaned against the bonnet.

'I thought you said you'd arranged for us to see this Newcomb woman, gov?'

'I didn't bloody well make it up,' Hamilton replied sarcastically. 'It's pretty obvious she's given me the run around.'

'Stinks of guilt, that does.'

Hamilton frowned. 'More lies, anyway. Let's drive round to the local police station, see if the local PCs can at least keep an eye out for Newcomb's car while they're patrolling the area.'

'I'll call Fraser while we're en route, and ask her to get the licence registration in advance.'

'Great idea. Better if we can supply them with as much information as possible, if we're asking for their assistance. Also, tell Fraser I want Newcomb added to the list of potential suspects, and we'll need the woman's full background checks done too.'

Hamilton thumped the steering wheel with the heel of his hand as he sat in the driver's seat. The investigation had begun to slip through his fingers, and DCI Allen's warning rung in his ears as loud as Big Ben's hourly chimes. Too many crimes were committed in London on a daily basis. If he couldn't obtain substantial evidence soon, his team would be forced to move onto another case.

CHAPTER SIXTEEN

Felicity drove away from Calvin's estate, the group's conversations replaying over and over again in her mind. They'd all finally agreed; their safest bet was to avoid the police and make an effort to find Donna themselves. Deciding their best course of action was to each take a few days' annual leave from work, they'd divided the tasks between themselves. She would use her contacts in the press, those who worked closely with the missing persons department. As Holly worked from home, she vowed to research local homeless shelters and contact them with Donna's details. Todd and Calvin promised to pair-up and visit associates they'd made during their university days. A long shot, they all concurred, especially with the years passed, but it was all they had.

Holly fiddled with the radio, flicking through stations faster than The Flash, and Felicity soon regretted offering her friend a lift home. But when Holly explained her car had broken down that morning, she hated the thought of her alone at night on public transport. She could sense Holly's eyes continually peaking over in her direction, and could hear the occasional sharp intake of breath.

'Spit it out, Hols.'

'Well, are you going to tell me what happened between you and Todd?'

'Nothing. What do you mean?' Felicity replied abruptly.

Holly giggled. 'Oh, come on, don't mug me off. When I couldn't find Calvin last night, I drove back round to your house. The bedroom light was on, but neither of you answered the door. And tonight …' Holly blew a loud, sharp whistle. 'The tension between the pair of you was bloody intense.'

Felicity rolled her eyes. She'd forgotten how much Holly could pick up on, even while looking uninterested. 'He tried to kiss me … well, he did kiss me, kind of. Anyway, I told him to sling his hook.'

'Ah ha,' her friend said, with raised eyebrows. 'I bet he didn't like that.'

'Well, no, I guess nobody would.'

'Flick, this is Todd we're talking about. He's always loved you, don't try and deny it. It must have squashed his heart when he found out about you and Warren getting engaged.'

She sighed. 'Yeah, well … I never felt *that* way about him, and I always made it clear. Don't go rubbing salt in old wounds now.'

Holly lifted her hands, posing surrender. 'Hey, I'm saying nothing more on the subject.'

A bright light distracted Felicity. The oncoming car flashed its headlights before racing by, well over the speed limit. Momentarily blinded, she raised an arm to shield her vision. Holly angrily shouted a few obscenities, not that the driver could hear her, Felicity thought. As she turned the corner, driving through a residential neighbourhood, she watched the car perform a U-turn in the road and speed up behind them.

'Fucking hell, Hols, the car's coming back after us.'

'Don't be such a drama queen. It's probably just kids messing around. Slow down and let the bastards drive on by.'

Felicity followed Holly's instructions and assumed the car would overtake, but instead the silhouette behind the wheel shunted into the back of her car. She pressed hard on the accelerator, speeding down the quiet road; her white knuckles gripped the steering wheel. The dark vehicle behind them mirrored her speed until they were bumper to bumper.

Holly twisted around in her seat. 'I can't see who it is, or how many are in the car, it's too dark.'

Her friend's shaky voice reflected the fear which now grabbed tight on to her chest. As she reached forty miles per hour, Felicity's eyes darted from left to right, desperate for an annoyed home owner to come out. But as they continued to drive, they reached the last house, and either side of their view was replaced by greenery and trees. The full moon shone onto an opening in the road; she could continue straight or turn around at the island and double back on herself. Holly's yells filled the car now, but Felicity couldn't make sense of what she said.

The attacking car jerked into Felicity once again, thrusting her further down the road. Guided by the light of the moon, she braked hard and spun right around the island. Attempting to stay on the road, she lost control of the car and smashed into the large trunk of an oak tree. She whirled around just in time to see the mysterious vehicle continue straight.

'What the fuck!' Holly yelled.

'Get out of the car.'

'What? Why?'

'Let's say my parking isn't what it used to be. I'm pretty sure nose-diving into a tree isn't the way it works, Hols.' She twisted the key in the ignition to be met with a low rumbling from the engine; the car well and truly asleep. 'We ain't going anywhere in this thing anyway, and what if that maniac returns?'

The sound of a perfectly working engine could be heard revving in the distance. Felicity grabbed the keys from the ignition and screamed at Holly again. She clicked the lock button while she ran away from the car and down the road.

'Wait for me,' Holly panted. 'This body wasn't built to run. My chest feels like it's on fire.'

'Someone is chasing us. We just need to get to the last house we passed. It can't be too far,' she yelled over her shoulder.

A piercing scream filled the silent street, and Felicity froze. The blackness of the night blinded her, offering only a limited vision as she slowly turned around to face her friend. Holly lay on the floor, screeching, the pain evident on her pale face.

Felicity rushed back to her. 'What happened?'

'I tripped. My ankle is busted.' Holly pulled herself up, yelping the entire time, and leaned back onto the iron fence separating the park from the road.

The roar of the car engine moved closer. The dimness of the headlights came into view. Felicity held her breath, as the black vehicle glided towards them and then screeched away again. Its two red backlights glowered out of the darkness like the devil disappearing into hell. She exhaled.

'They're just fucking with us, Flick,' Holly stuttered. 'I told you. It's just kids messing around.'

Unconvinced, Felicity glanced up and down, the hotness in her chest taking over. 'Okay, have you got your mobile?'

'Yes.'

'I left mine in my handbag in the car. Do you think you could hobble back?'

'To the car?'

'Yes!' Felicity snapped, peering back to her dented car.

'Oh, Flick, I don't know.'

'Holly, stop being an idiot. This is *deadly* serious. When will you realise that?' Holly's discomfort was clear, and Felicity almost felt sorry for shouting. But as the grumble of the car returned, she realised they were in no position to take any chances. She grabbed her friend's hand. 'Listen, take the keys and hop like mad back to the car. Lock yourself in, and call the police immediately. We're not far from Calvin's place, a few miles, if that.'

'What about you?'

'I'm going to carry on back to the houses. Someone has to answer the door. From there, I can ring 999 and get the location from the home owner. With everything that's happened, we can't be too cautious.' Felicity's voice didn't waver, despite her legs feeling as unsteady as a new born deer.

Holly finally agreed, and she helped guide her friend away from the fence. Holly stood unaided, one foot taking all her weight, the other foot hanging awkwardly inches in the air. Felicity pressed the keys into her hand, and before the tears in Holly's eyes could stop her, she turned and raced away.

* * *

Felicity shrieked as the iconic Scream face came into full view. She immediately recognised the person behind the mask had to be someone who knew her well. Only those close to her understood the terror that gripped her when confronted with the white, elongated ghost face and the black emptiness of a mouth and eyes.

She remembered one Halloween party, and the Brunel campus rife with students dressed in the iconic attire. The black material flew in the wind as the wearer wildly ran from student union to halls of residence, wielding a fake knife. Most onlookers had screeched and yelped, but laughed and encouraged the behaviour all the same. Felicity froze, the fear paralysed her to the spot. She'd thrown up the first time she'd watched the movie, and since then, never again watched a horror film. The thought of not knowing who, or what, was behind the cloak of darkness made her stomach turn.

Now, the panic rose in her chest and lodged in her throat. She could barely breathe. Her shouts for help were mere croaks. The wearer of the mask smiled underneath, of that she was certain; no one dressed in a disguise made of pure evil without gaining pleasure for themselves. The urine leaked through her underwear and trickled down her thigh. It was only then she noticed the ropes strapped to her wrists and ankles, firmly securing her to a wooden table.

The coldness whipped around, while the stinking damp travelled up her nostrils. She strained to take in the surroundings. Dim, but just enough light shone from behind her to illuminate the tall figure lingering over her. The dirty, small windows and low, wooden beams revealed she must be trapped in some kind of shed, or outhouse. The tears gushed silently as she gasped for air.

The costumed figure stepped forward. Gloved hands peeked out of the black robes and picked up various instruments from the metal stand next to Felicity. The ghost face tilted slowly from one side to the other, examining the different tools on offer.

'Why are you doing this?' Felicity whispered. 'Donna, I know it's you … it is, isn't it? I'll understand, I'm sure I can help you … but let's talk about this first.'

Ghost face laid down the instruments and bent over Felicity. She closed her eyes, willing her captor away. Warm breath escaped the mesh mask and flooded her face. She whimpered.

'Please, Donna, just tell me what you want. You don't have to hurt me.'

'I want answers!' yelled a distorted voice.

Felicity clamped her eyes shut further, realising ghost face had the same voice changer the killer used in the film. Her nightmare had come alive.

'I … I don't understand,' she stuttered. 'Why? And … What about Holly? Did you …'

'That bitch has been taken care of, don't worry.'

The sobs caught in Felicity's throat. A long, rumbling sigh travelled through the device and out of the mask, before her abductor stood and grabbed her left hand.

'Journalists need their fingers, don't they?' Ghost Face sneered. 'How about I cut one off every time you don't answer a question?' The tears continued to flow while Felicity's hand was squashed together with such force, she thought the bones inside would break. 'You must hear so many different stories and gossip … trying to make yourself famous by other people's misfortune.'

Felicity felt the sharp tip of a needle pierce her arm. Her own screams echoed throughout the room. Sweat dripped from her forehead, while her heart raced like a drummer.

'What. What are you doing? Why?' she mumbled.

'Now, we wouldn't want you passing out too early, would we?' the distorted voice said. The monster placed Felicity's baby finger inside a pair of plyers. 'We'll start small. I need to know what really happened at Lake Windermere.'

'Please don't do this,' she urged. 'Donna, if that is you under the mask, I know you really don't want to do this. Please, things weren't meant to play out like they did. It was a stupid dare. You were up for it –'

'Shut up! You know nothing.'

The steel clamped through Felicity's flesh and bone. Distorted yells pieced her eardrums, her eyes rolled back into her head. She begged the assailant to stop, promising she knew nothing more.

'You just can't stop yourself from lying!' the low voice boomed, travelling around the table and injecting Felicity's right arm. 'Treat people like utter shit, that's what you've always done. Take no responsibility for your actions. What about all the pain you caused your friends? You're a low-life slag.'

'No. Please.'

'If only you'd been honest with me.'

'I will. I will,' Felicity repeated, desperate to look down at her hand where blood gushed from the exposed, cold wound.

'Maybe this will help you.'

Ghost face lifted a transparent bucket from the ground. Felicity's eyes widened and she thrashed around the wooden table at the sight of hundreds of spiders, all different shapes and sizes, climbing over each other. An evil laugh reverberated through the hidden device.

'No! Please. No!'

The gloved hand lifted the lid from the container and launched its contents over Felicity's torso and legs. She immediately felt the whispers of their legs scurrying over her skin. Some up her trousers and others crawled towards her neck. She threw her head from left to right, hoping to propel some of them from her body, but the movement came much slower, as though her petrified body had begun to give up on her. Scared to open her mouth, she lay bound and snivelling.

Ghost Face snorted. 'Oh, yes, another Felicity fear. You really should be careful the secrets you divulge with your *friends*. Especially if you intend on stabbing them in the back one day.'

A spider bit Felicity's inner thigh. She arched her back and lifted her buttocks, struggling to shift the eight-legged creatures, but hoping to squash a few of them as she thumped back down onto the table.

Am I moving at all?

Throwing her head back, she thought of her mum, her sister, and her niece, wondering if she'd ever see them again. A low howl escaped her lips.

'Shut up!' the voice demanded. 'Now, I want the truth, before it's too late for you to answer. Tell me exactly what happened during that trip to Ambleside two years ago.'

CHAPTER SEVENTEEN

Two years ago

Felicity gripped the mobile phone between her fingers and nervously searched through the crowded library. As coursework deadlines loomed, and with exams imminent, it became the only time the campus's old building would be busier than the bar. Studying came naturally to Felicity, a trait many of her friends had come to hate over the years. But she enjoyed learning and somehow managed to learn a lot with minimal effort. She could retain information she'd only read or heard once, regardless of years passing, and she valued absorbing new things. Research, to Felicity, was fun, entertaining, and rewarding. It was the main reason she'd chosen journalism as her degree; having the chance to delve into new things and people, as well as historical and unexplained events, enthralled her. But she also understood that wasn't the case for everyone, especially with nerve-wracking exams around the corner.

She scanned each passage between the towering, mahogany bookcases and prayed she'd find her friend. The text message she'd received just twenty minutes previously, while on the bus intu Uxbridge town centre, worried her. She'd jumped off at the next stop and jogged back to campus. As she approached the backend of the second floor, she wondered if she'd need to search the other levels of the building, or if maybe she hadn't been quick enough in returning to the library.

'There you are,' she exclaimed, and rushed down the last passage, an echo of shushing from fellow students in her wake. 'What's happened?'

Donna sat slumped on the floor, her back against the hard wood, the shelves almost bare of resources. Her head rested on her knees, strands of honey-blonde hair sticking to her wet cheeks. Felicity slid beside her and scooped her up into a bear hug. It felt like hours before Donna finally lifted her head and faced Felicity, a rim of swollen redness surrounded her friend's eyes.

'What am I going to do, Flick?' Donna whispered.

She lowered her tone to match her friends, and to keep the high-on-caffeine students from lynching her for making too much noise. 'Your text made no sense, Donna. What do you mean you can't cope with anything anymore?'

Donna wiped her face, brushing the remnants of tears into her hair. 'I've left everything to the last minute, Flick. All the books I need are already out on loan; I'll never get them in time to finish my dissertation. I've screwed up. I'm never going to graduate now.'

Felicity's chest tightened, as her friend's head fell down into her lap. She'd never witnessed Donna so low; usually the life and soul of any party, there'd never been a sign of worry for assignments.

'D, you have started your dissertation, right?' Felicity held her breath, too worried to miss the answer.

'Of course.' A muffled noise came from Felicity's thighs, and she lightly pulled Donna's head up. 'I don't even have much more to write, but the resources I need aren't here. How can they only have a few flaming copies of certain important books in this enormous place?'

As Donna's tone rose higher than anyone in the library would be happy with, Felicity guided her onto her feet and towards the door. Students crammed together at the large tables, or stood in queues for the photocopiers and computers. Felicity silently mimed her apologies as she barged through them with Donna clinging to her arm like a drunk person.

Despite the fresh air, Donna dropped to the bottom step and sat down with a sigh. Felicity yearned to help her friend, but she knew nothing about creative writing. She was a woman who stuck purely to the facts when creating her stories. Her concerns were interrupted by Calvin, who yelled their names as he exited the bar, directly opposite the library.

'What's with the long faces?' he asked. 'Don't tell me you're joining my club, and they've kicked you out of university. Jeez, not far off graduation too. That's hard luck.'

Felicity punched him in the arm and shook her head, hoping he'd get the hint and leave them alone. But it was too late; Donna jumped to her feet in seconds.

'You'd fucking love that, wouldn't you, Cal? Then you wouldn't be the only loser around here. Why are you still here anyway?'

Calvin flinched, a mixture of confusion and pain stamped on his face. 'It was a joke.'

'My degree is really important to me,' Donna continued, and took a step closer to Calvin, his towering figure peered down at her petite and wild face. 'It's not my fault I'm not being supplied with the right tools I need to get the job done … What do you care? You don't understand.'

He raised his hands in protest as Donna elbowed him out of the way. Felicity felt torn, there were now two of her closest friends feeling less than their normal selves. But she knew Calvin could bounce back, and it wasn't the first time Donna had blown off steam at one of them.

'What the actual fuck was that about, Flick?'

'Forget it, mate,' she said and walked backwards away from him. 'Just dissertation stuff, you wouldn't get it.'

As she turned to catch up with Donna, Felicity regretted her choice of words and hoped Calvin wouldn't take them as another low blow. She promised herself she'd buy him a pint later and explain. The two women walked away from campus, towards the bus stop, when a thought occurred to Felicity.

'Hey, you said your dissertation was about realism in creative writing, or something like that, didn't you?'

Donna nodded solemnly. 'Essentially, yes. It's more in depth than that with different topics and styles of writing, but I'm examining how different aspects of reality are entwined into non-fiction novels. The last book I needed … well, you know the rest.' She puffed out her cheeks and exhaled loudly.

'What about journalism? I've got tons of resource books on the subject back at my flat, and maybe you could focus on a book that –'

'*In Cold Blood*,' Donna screamed, and jumped up and down on the spot. 'Flipping hell, Flick! Truman Capote followed the lives of those murderers in Kansas, interviewing their families, as well as the victims and their families. All before he wrote a single word of the actual book, which can be argued is a mix of fiction and non-fiction. His story was completely influenced. I could go so many different ways with this. What a frigging awesome idea.'

Felicity couldn't contain clapping along with Donna's eagerness, until the moment she caught her reflection in a nearby window and realised they both resembled performing seals. She corrected herself and walked on, with Donna now happily jabbering away beside her. It wasn't the evening Felicity had envisioned, but she invited Donna back to her apartment and offered help scouring through her personal library of textbooks.

'Look, while we're at it tonight, why don't we book a weekend away for us all after graduation?' she suggested, deciding they all needed a break after the strenuous final year of studies. 'That way, you'll have something to look forward to after all the extra hours you'll need to put in for your dissertation.'

'Hell yeah, I'm up for that. We should all get away together, you're right. You really are the best friend a girl could ask for, did you know that?' Donna said and linked her arm through Felicity's. 'What would I bloody do without you, woman?'

She smiled. 'Luckily, we'll never have to find out.'

CHAPTER EIGHTEEN

Hamilton marched into the incident room, greeted by the usual whirl of printers and computers, numerous conversations over the phones and between colleagues, and the gurgle of the boiling kettle in the far corner. Clarke strutted through the office and yanked the chair from under his desk, his face as disappointed as Hamilton felt.

Fraser barely acknowledged them, except for a quick wave, as she ran her fingers through her hair, drawing it away from her face. Her fingers worked speedily over the keyboard, while her eyes bore into the screen. Despite being occupied on the phone, Rocky's face flashed with his signature grin. Hoping the call wasn't a personal one, Hamilton couldn't refrain from smiling himself; the young lad's cheeky chappie routine was infectious. Dixon slurped another mouthful of coffee before standing up and rounding the desks to meet Hamilton at the evidence boards.

'Just in time, boss,' she said. 'I was about to update the information.'

'Great, what have we got so far?'

'I've been looking into the group's academic studies at Brunel and found something interesting about Calvin Robinson.' Dixon placed a hand on her hip and read from a sheet of paper. 'While Robinson did attend the university, he failed the first year of his journalism course. He didn't reapply, or re-sit any exams, or resubmit any coursework, from what I can ascertain. Rocky's on the phone to someone at the uni now, trying to gather more details for me.'

'Interesting, considering Robinson joined the rest of his friends on a graduation celebration trip,' Hamilton mused.

'Perhaps he transferred to a different university,' Clarke offered.

Dixon shrugged. 'We'll soon find out. Anyway, we dug further into the group's background. While Warren and Felicity had quite a normal upbringing ... well, as *normal* as anyone can, I suppose, that can't be said for the other three. Holly Walker's mother overdosed, and the girl was placed into social care, before being adopted at the age of fifteen. Todd Bell lost both his parents in the London 7/7 bombings in 2005. He was twelve.' Dixon paused for a moment, inhaled a large breath and continued. 'Bell then lived with his grandmother, even during his uni years. When she passed away last year, he inherited the house and currently lives there. Lastly, Calvin Robinson, also placed into social care after his mother was arrested for prostitution, however, he was never adopted and bounced from foster home to foster home until the age of eighteen. Robinson also served a stint in Feltham, the Young Offender Institution, when he was fifteen for theft and possession of cannabis. By some stroke of luck, he secured a place at Brunel through Clearings.'

Hamilton exhaled loudly. 'Okay, this is what we needed. I feel like I'm actually getting a picture of these people now. Good. Get these notes up for everyone to see, and I'd also like a print-out of all this so I can read over it again.'

'Sure thing, boss,' Dixon said and busied herself at the evidence boards as Rocky joined them.

'Calvin Robinson did not reapply to Brunel, or transfer to another university,' Rocky explained. 'He did, however, continue working in the bar on campus for the last two years of the course.'

'While his friends were still studying their degrees?' Clarke questioned.

'Yes. I can't find out where he lived during those two years, but after they'd graduated, Robinson moved to the studio flat he currently resides in, and began working at the coffee shop where we first met him.'

Hamilton nodded. 'And were any of them studying science, or medical related degrees?'

'No, boss. Including Donna Moran, it was two for journalism, two for creative writing, film and TV studies, and social work. Fraser's delved into their personal and working lives more.'

'Good work,' Hamilton announced, and watched the gleam in Rocky's hazel eyes at the praise he'd received from his superior. 'Mirror Dixon's actions and keep everyone updated. I want a hardcopy of everything we've got so far.'

Once he had the information from the two newest recruits, and he'd updated them about Claire Newcomb's deceit, Hamilton dismissed the three of them and waited for Fraser. He quickly checked his mobile, pleased to find a positive reply from Elizabeth about his suggestion of staying with her mother. He could now spend the evening uncovering what had happened to their security lights at home.

'Sorry, boss, but I wanted to make sure I had everything I could find. I know you wanted to make progress this evening,' Fraser finally spoke, and pushed away from her desk. 'Don't worry, I heard everything you all said, so I'm up to speed with everything. And I've printed out the info I've got so far, for the personal file you're creating.'

He was in awe of the young Sergeant, and her ability to multi-task without letting her own work slip. However, on closer inspection, he began to worry about her; her porcelain face had adopted a grey tinge, the heavy bags under her blue eyes were startlingly apparent, and she'd yawned at least a dozen times since his return.

'At the moment, I can't find any direct connection with the group of friends and Botox suppliers or distributers,' Fraser continued. 'However, I now have further knowledge of a few family members, as well as Melanie King, the woman Todd Bell is dating. So, I'm going to delve straight into them.'

'Not this evening you're not,' Hamilton said and leaned over to switch off her computer monitor.

'Have I done something wrong?'

'No, you've done everything right … except look after yourself, maybe.' Hamilton paused. 'Is there anything you want to discuss with me, Fraser?'

She curved her lips downwards and shook her head. 'No, boss. Everything's fine.' He frowned and waited for more. 'I guess I could do with a bit more sleep most nights … but couldn't we all?'

'Last week, when I returned from my weekend away, you mentioned wanting to have a chat with me.'

Fraser waved a hand in the air, dismissing his comment. 'It's all sorted now, boss. Honestly, everything is fine.'

Hamilton sighed. 'Well, if you're sure? You know I'm always here, if you need to discuss anything.' She nodded silently, and he knew nothing more would be shared tonight. 'Head home, catch up on some well-deserved sleep, and I'll see you first thing in the morning.'

'I thought you wanted to make a decision about this group of friends.'

He held up the file in his hand. 'I'm going to take this home now and get all the information together in my mind.'

* * *

Hamilton pushed open the car door and froze when its movement alerted the security beam. His front garden illuminated. He remained statue-like, in a half-in, half-out of the car crouching position, and studied his house. The living room curtains had been drawn together, but no glimmer of light escaped through the small crack in the middle. A glow from the upstairs window told him the lamp in his bedroom had been switched on. Leaving the door open, he eased himself from the driver's seat and silently approached the front door. He waited, with his head down, and listened intently through the wooden door. The surrounding sounds of cars and pedestrians faded into background noise. Gliding the key into the lock, he gently pushed the front door open and took a large stride inside.

An angelic voice reached his ears, the smell of bacon wafted up his nostrils, and he exhaled a sigh of relief. He stepped inside the kitchen and smiled. Leaning against the doorway, he folded his arms and watched his wife shake her hips from side to side while belting out an Adele tune. He wolf-whistled, causing her to scream as she spun around and threw the kitchen towel at him.

'You scared the bloody life out of me, Denis!' Elizabeth shrieked. 'How long have you been standing there?'

He reached down and lifted the kitchen towel from the floor. 'Long enough to see you've got some new moves, Mrs Hamilton.' He laughed when she rolled her eyes and turned her attention back to the dinner. 'What are you doing here anyway?'

'I live here.' She lowered the gas on the cooker and closed the distance between them. 'When you tell me to stay at my mother's house, I know something's up.'

'So, you lied in your text message and just ignored my request?'

Elizabeth winked. 'Pretty much. Denis, if there's a problem, I want to know about it. Don't push me away.'

'I'm not. But a few things bugged me, and I just wanted to make sure you were safe.' He paused and frowned. 'Actually, how are the security lights working again?'

'I checked the internal power switch, and it had been turned off. Must have been me when I reached inside the cupboards to get the cleaning stuff out the other day.'

Hamilton flung his head back and laughed out loud. 'I'm a bloody idiot.'

'Old age that is, Denis, if you're spooked by the lights not working.'

Elizabeth turned away, and Hamilton slapped her across the arse. 'Less of the old. I'm not even forty.'

'Only a few more months, old-timer. Listen, I've run a bath for myself, so I'm off for a long soak. If you eat up quick, I may even wait for you in there.' She kissed him on the cheek, left the kitchen and climbed the stairs.

'Now there's an offer an old man can't refuse,' he shouted.

Remembering the car was still unlocked, Hamilton stepped outside the house. He swooped inside and placed his hand on the case file left on the passenger's seat. Crunching gravel from behind forced him to turn around and come face to face with a tall, white man. He grabbed the stranger by the neck and swung him onto the car.

The man threw his hands in the air. 'Hey, calm down! Don't shoot, it's me. It's Billy.'

Hamilton relaxed his hold, but didn't entirely release his grip. He stared into the man's face, and his brow knit together. He then recognised Billy's light green eyes and cropped black hair, but the man had aged in the four years since they'd seen each other last. There were whispers of grey hairs in Billy's short, shaven beard. The deep wrinkles on his forehead and around his eyes creased his white skin. But Hamilton had to admit, his friend also looked tons better than he did before.

'You're not going to shoot me, right?' Billy repeated.

'I don't have a gun, you idiot,' Hamilton spat back, and finally let go. 'Why are you saying that? Have you done something so bad you deserved to be shot at?'

Billy straightened his clothes. 'No. But you look pretty pissed.'

'As would you, if strangers crept up behind you.'

He might as well have punched Billy in the stomach. The man's shoulders slumped, and he looked down at the ground, his left foot dancing along the gravel as he tucked his hands in his jeans pockets. Hamilton sighed, recalling the insecure pose his old friend would adopt whenever he felt attacked by someone.

'Jesus, what are you doing here, Billy? You were here the other night too, weren't you? I chased you down the road. Have you been watching me?'

Billy's head shot up. 'Yes, okay … I guess I've been "watching you,"' he said, his fingers making quotation signs in the air. 'But only because I need to talk to you, Den. I wanted to make sure you still lived here and …'

'And what, Billy? I haven't heard from you in years, now you're skulking around my house looking for my help. Where were you when I needed *your* help? When I needed my best mate.'

Billy glanced away. 'I know … I've made some decisions I'm not proud of, Den. Yes, I've been AWOL for a while, but I can explain all that. My life is completely different now, and I want you to be a part of it again. Give me a chance to explain everything, mate.'

Their conversation was interrupted by the piercing ringtone of Hamilton's mobile. He shook his head, pulled the phone from his inner jacket pocket, and turned away from Billy.

'DI Hamilton,' he answered, and listened to the instructions from the station sergeant.

The body of a young female had been found in the River Thames, next to the Embankment Pier. The sergeant continued to explain, with DI Delaney busy attending another scene, his presence was requested.

'I'm just about to call DS Clarke, sir, and inform him of the situation. Shall I phone the rest of your team?' the sergeant asked.

'No, not at this time, thank you. Are SOCO at the scene already?'

'They're en route, sir. The area was cordoned off twenty minutes ago, by the attending officers.'

'Thanks, I'm on my way.'

He disconnected the call and turned around. Despite his meek manner, Hamilton glanced over Billy's large physique for the first time, surprised at how much the man had bulked out over the years. Billy's slender frame had been replaced with hefty arms and an enormous chest. He wasn't the man Hamilton had remembered.

'Sounds like you're needed,' Billy said, his sad eyes met Hamilton's.

'Yeah … duty calls and all that.'

Hamilton jingled the keys in his hand, waiting for Billy to move from his resting position against the car. Plagued by the past, and unsure what to say to this stranger – his friend since the age of eleven – he thought of the boy who had needed saving from the bullies. The teenager who had helped Hamilton with his homework. The man who had been godfather to his daughter.

'Come on, move out the way, Billy. I have to go.'

His friend nodded and stepped away from the door. 'I know. I get what you do is important, but please say you'll meet me for a drink, Den. I really want to have a chat with you.'

Hamilton hesitated, but knew his own curiosity would always get the better of him. 'Fine. I'll meet you, Billy. Tomorrow night?'

'Yeah, lovely. What about at The Duck in the Pond? Our old haunt … though I don't think we know anyone in there anymore. I'll be there from eight.'

Billy beamed while they arranged their next meet-up, but Hamilton couldn't reciprocate the man's delight. When a person from your past crawled out of the shadows, after all those years, there was more to it than just wanting a chat, he thought. Nevertheless, he had to push those thoughts to be back of his mind; a woman had been murdered on the streets of London, and that was where his concentration needed to be right now.

Hamilton slammed the car door shut, started the ignition, and switched the siren on. Although he felt guilty not explaining his departure to Elizabeth, he knew she'd understand; it wasn't the first time he'd had to race off to work at a moment's notice. As he reversed from his driveway at breakneck speed, he spied Billy in the rear-view mirror watching him race away from his home.

CHAPTER NINETEEN

The blue whirlwind of the police cars sirens lit up the Embankment like a neon party. It attracted London's late-night revellers and tourists, who stood behind the crime scene tape with their phones primed for photographs and Facebook live streaming. Hamilton barged through the insensitive crowd. The fury bubbled so close to the surface, his skin ablaze with anger. He quickly flashed his ID badge and was permitted entrance to the crime scene.

Uniformed police, stationed at the bridge entrance of the pier, ensured Hamilton stopped to sign the log book held by a portly constable. Once over the bridge, he found the forensic team already in full motion. He slipped on the compulsory shoe covers and walked further along the boat. The victim's body had been transported to the inside enclosure of the Pier, away from the prying eyes of passers-by, and head pathologist, Laura Joseph, was in the process of recording her findings.

'Hello, Inspector,' Laura said and clicked the stop button on her digital voice recorder. 'No identification at the moment, but the body was found forty-minutes ago by one of the river cruise workers. Your partner is having a chat with him at the other end of the Pier. The witness was walking across the bridge and saw our victim floating in the river between the Pier and the wall. We've not long removed her from the water.'

Hamilton peered along the pier. Formed like a glass tunnel, with stunning views of the Thames and Hungerford Bridge, it was one of the city's most popular hubs for river boats; with hop-on, hop-off cruises and river bus services to attractions such as Tower Bridge and The O2. He located Clarke, towering above a pockmarked faced young man wearing a Crown River Cruises cap.

'So, she was dumped in the Thames?'

Laura stood from her crouching position and mockingly rolled her eyes. 'One day, Inspector Hamilton, you'll let me do my job before the interrogation begins. You know anything I tell you here at the scene is unfounded until the post-mortem.'

'I know, I know. But, Jesus, I can't sit on my heels for days waiting for your reports. Anything you tell me here is only used to send me off in, hopefully, the right direction. I'm a hound looking for a scent,' he said, with a sly smile. 'Plus, I've got another hard-hitting investigation I'm dealing with at the moment. So, come on ...'

She folded her arms across her chest, its athletic frame hidden by the white forensic suit swamping her body. 'From my brief observations, I can't calculate Jane Doe's exact cause of death, due to the obvious signs of torture. A large head laceration, various puncture marks dotted over her arms, ligature wounds around her neck, wrists and ankles, plus three fingers on her right hand were severed, I think ante-mortem.'

Hamilton exhaled noisily at the pathologist's description of the young woman's death. 'Could have been a clean-up tactic. If the victim fought back, she may have had his DNA under her fingernails.'

He could never fathom the evilness surging through the veins of some of the world's population. Those same people who sat next to you in a coffee shop, or on the bus to work, the delivery drivers who knocked on your door daily, or the waiter who served your dinner in a restaurant. Occasionally, the only way to catch a murderer was to empty your mind of everything and truly climb inside the mind of a killer, he thought. But at times like this, when Hamilton heard of the depraved and vile ways criminals hurt other human beings, he found it difficult to do anything but feel repulsed.

'How long are we talking, Laura?'

'Recent. Possibly within the last few hours. I can't be sure if the victim was discarded here, or further along and floated along the Pier, but I'd be willing to guess she's only been in the water for an hour, maybe a little more.'

'I'd say her killer would be pretty stupid to have discarded her at this location, what with all the surrounding bar and restaurant boats also moored along here,' Hamilton pondered, scanning the length of the Pier again and examining everything around him in detail.

Laura squatted back down and grabbed the white sheet covering the woman's body. 'Well, let's hope stupid is exactly what your killer is, if you want to get back to your other case.'

She yanked back the shroud from the victim's head, and Hamilton's shoulders slumped. 'Looks like the two could be connected, Laura. This woman's name is Felicity Ireland, and she *is* part of my other investigation.'

He gazed down at Felicity's slick face. The water hadn't attacked her features beyond recognition yet, nor did the purple swollenness of her left eye hinder Hamilton's ability to identify the victim. But a grimy coating from the Thames shadowed her face. Her blonde hair, wet and matted, with dark blood mixed into the strands. The pink softness of her full lips had drained away, replaced with the grey cracks of death. Hamilton caught a glimpse of a colourful hummingbird on a piece of silk material peeking out from under the white forensic blanket.

'Have you checked inside her mouth?' he asked, with a sigh.

The pathologist frowned. 'No.'

'Could you please?'

With gloved hands, Laura carefully pulled down Felicity's chin and revealed the tip of a foreign item inside the victim's mouth. She motioned for a member of the SOCO team to join her, and the young man raced around the body, taking photographs. The camera clicks and flashes of light bellowed like an air raid warning in Hamilton's ears. Laura used a similar tool to the one he'd seen in Ambleside, placed it into Felicity's mouth, and cautiously pulled out a piece of crumpled paper.

Hamilton clenched his jaw. 'Is the name Donna Moran written on it?'

Laura glanced up and nodded, and he quickly updated the woman on the Speed and Moran investigations. As he finished, Clarke approached and explained the teenage witness, Liam Osborne, had found the body after he'd finished his shift on the Pier. Unfortunately, Liam hadn't heard, or seen, anything else out of the ordinary, but would give them the surveillance CDs from the river bus's cameras.

'Good, we'll definitely need those, Clarke … that's Felicity Ireland they've just extracted from the Thames,' he said and balled his fists.

If Dixon was right, and these friends were the victims as opposed to the suspects, he'd let this woman suffer by not protecting her. He'd allowed his gut instinct, that they were somehow involved in the murder and disappearance of their friends, lead his decision to not warn them all of a potential threat.

'Right, call the team in,' Hamilton commanded. 'I want those CDs and the surrounding CCTV footage examined as a top priority. Felicity Ireland wasn't placed in the river long ago; there's still a chance we can catch where this guy went. I've got the case file in my car, we'll head straight over to her next of kin.'

* * *

In the large family room, where Hamilton explained the evening's events to Dorinda Ireland, he watched the woman fall to her knees and scream until her throat dried of all saliva. He slipped a hand under her arm and helped her up onto the plump, grey corduroy sofa. He remembered the moment his world shattered, the heaviness in his chest when he tried to breathe, so he allowed Dorinda to rest her head on his shoulder.

'Is there anyone we can call for you, Miss Ireland?' Clarke asked from where he stood opposite them. His eyes glazed for just a moment.

Dorinda snivelled and shook her head. 'My partner should be home soon; he went out for a few drinks with a friend after work.'

'Is there anyone else in the house with you?'

The woman jumped up and stood in the doorway, her ear cocked in the direction of the stairs. 'My daughter, Amelia. She's only two. I hope I didn't disturb her … oh god!' She clutched her hands together and stumbled against the bookshelf. 'What am I going to tell Amelia? Aunty City … that's what she calls Felicity … was her best friend. She adored my sister. She always had time for my little baby, her little niece, and I … I just …'

Silent sobs broke through Dorinda's ramblings and Hamilton, once again, guided her to the sofa. He nodded at Clarke, an unspoken suggestion to make the grieving woman a strong cup of coffee. It wasn't exactly something he'd want at this time, but the gestures of strangers went a long way when you were at your lowest.

'Dorinda, we've arranged a Family Liaison Officer for you. They will be here shortly. In the meantime, and I hate to do this right now, but did Felicity confide in you? Was there anything she was worried about? Had anyone been following her, or in contact with her lately?'

'Erm … no,' she said and repeatedly shook her head. 'I mean, Warren, of course. That's the only thing on her mind at the moment … *was* the only thing. That's all we spoke about this past week … you can image. Why? Why Felicity … how could this happen? Jesus Christ, is this related to Warren's murder. Of course, it is. I mean, it is, isn't it?'

'We believe there is a strong connection, yes. It's definitely the route we're taking the investigation at the moment.'

Hamilton followed the woman's gaze to a photograph on the mantelpiece of Felicity's graduation day. There, in full cap and gown, the young woman was surrounded by her five friends, Calvin the only person not in the ceremonial robes.

'I was so proud of her that day,' Dorinda whispered. 'Our mum was in a residential home by then, God bless her, but Felicity had graduated with honours and was set on her career in journalism. I'd given birth to Amelia a few weeks before … William and I were at our happiest … we all were. Isn't it cruel, how in just one moment everything can change forever? Your whole life …' She clicked her fingers. 'Gone.'

Clarke reappeared and placed the cup in front of Dorinda. Her eyes remained fixed ahead, the redness around them growing as the silent tears continued to run down her cheeks.

'This is a very difficult time, I understand that,' Hamilton said. 'But if there's anything you can think of that might help us catch Felicity's killer, we'd really appreciate it.'

Dorinda shrugged and then howled, letting her head fall into her hands. For her, it wasn't the time for this discussion; Hamilton recognised that only too well. He also knew his time would be better spent with his team tracking down the violent bastard. So, he explained to Dorinda they had to leave.

'As I said, the FLO will be here shortly –'

'It's fine, you can go,' she mumbled. 'I'm okay … William will be home soon. And the family person … Fine.'

Hamilton squeezed Dorinda's shoulder as he and Clarke left the room. Outside, the pair jumped in their separate cars with the intention of heading back to the station. As he turned the key in the ignition, a man in a black suit turned onto the road and made his way along Dorinda Ireland's driveway. Hamilton glanced in Clarke's direction, who gave him the thumbs up before pulling away from the kerb. Certain his partner assumed the stranger was the FLO, Hamilton puffed his cheeks as the reality of the situation dawned on him. The man in the suit was not an employee of the Met Police.

CHAPTER TWENTY

'An engaged couple, both brutally tortured and murdered. The fact they were both found in the water, *iconic* bodies of water for that matter, can't be discounted. But why, what's the motive?' Hamilton questioned his team once they were all back together in the incident room. 'We haven't found any fingerprints, or other DNA, so our suspect list is slimmer than a string bean. To be perfectly honest, I'm pissed off.'

'We feel your frustration, partner,' Clarke said and joined Rocky scouring the CCTV.

Dixon roughly flipped her dark hair over her head. 'This could be a crime of passion. While it's unlikely both would be murdered, the killer could have been caught up in an affair with either Warren Speed or Felicity Ireland. They were then dumped, shunned, and ignored. It's terrifying what jealously and rage can do to a person.'

'Fraser, what do you think?' Hamilton asked. 'Warren Speed was in the public eye; you seem to know a lot about his private life. Have you read any sort of expose in the papers along these lines?'

She shook her head. 'But let's not knock Dixon's theory, especially as I've been doing some digging into Claire Newcomb and discovered her brother, Jason, works for The Skin Clinic on Bond Street.'

Hamilton's heartbeat quickened. 'And I'm hoping you're going to continue by telling us it's some kind of cosmetic beauty clinic?'

'Correct. Its treatments include collagen injections, implants, and Botox. I'd guess there'd be plenty of vials on the premises.'

'Clarke, I want an APW sent out immediately. Hammersmith were given Claire Newcomb's car details, but I want all the local stations looking for her now. Rocky, keep your eyes peeled for a white Mini in the CCTV footage near and around the Embankment. Fraser, rush through a background check on this Jason. I don't want to miss anything. And Dixon, get in touch with Laura Joseph in the pathology department. Ask her to check if a high concentration of Botox was present in Felicity Ireland's body.'

The shrill of the office phone cut through his urgent demands. Surprised that the FLO assigned to Dorinda Ireland had contacted him at the office so soon, Hamilton perched on the desk.

'This is Lisa. I thought you should know Miss Ireland has just taken a call from Holly Walker, who claims she and two other friends were with Felicity last night,' the family liaison officer explained.

'Who were the other two friends?' Hamilton asked.

'Let me see …' she paused, briefly. 'Todd Bell and Calvin Robinson.'

He groaned. 'Well, of course, I should have seen that coming.'

'I suggested Miss Walker visit you to make a statement. She's on her way to Charing Cross Station now.'

'Excellent. Thank you for acting so quickly with this information, Lisa.'

Hamilton relayed the information to his team and set about making arrangements for the two males to also be brought in for questioning.

'I think it might be time to put your suggestion into play, Rocky.'

The young Constable hitched his shoulder and grinned. 'Oh yeah, and which one are you referring to, gov?'

'I want the three remaining friends in one place at the same time. But we won't give them a chance to all have a chin-wag – we'll split them up and interview them separately. I want to oversee everything, so I'll watch from the viewing room.'

Hamilton explained the line of questioning he wanted his team to take with each of the potential witnesses. It was imperative they finally gained an understanding of what had really happened to Donna Moran. Apart from the glaringly obvious clue, he believed the missing woman would lead them to the answers they needed to ensure another life wasn't stolen. He also had faith that by revealing another member of their group had been murdered, the three remaining friends would be alarmed and finally jolted into sharing their story.

* * *

Hamilton stood, his back straight and arms crossed over his chest, as he watched Fraser and Rocky explain the sequence of recent events to Holly Walker. The curvaceous young woman pulled a hand through her short, red hair. Her pale white skin was blotchy from using a screwed-up tissue to wipe the tears and mascara stains from her cheeks. Holly had learned of Felicity's demise after speaking to Dorinda Ireland.

'I was with her … it's my fault this has happened to Flick. If I'd made her stay with me … ' Holly stuttered through deep breaths.

'Calm down, Miss Walker, have a sip of this water,' Fraser said and lowered a plastic cup to the table. 'Slowly, tell us exactly what happened last night.'

'We left Calvin's house at about seven p.m., half an hour after Todd. We hadn't driven very far, maybe a few miles, when it was clear we were being followed. I didn't believe Flick at first; I truly believed it was pure paranoia. But it soon became obvious the person in the car was following us.'

'Can you remember what the car looked like, or did you see who was driving?' Rocky asked.

Holly shook her head. 'It was dark; I couldn't see the driver's face. But the car was black. A Ford Focus, same model as mine, except this one had tinted windows.'

She continued to describe what happened once Felicity was out of sight, and Hamilton's eyes roamed over every inch of her body – the shaking hands and twitching leg, and the constant snivelling into the tissue.

Holly cleared her throat. 'I managed to hobble back to the car, but my battery had died, so I couldn't call the police like she asked. I stuck the key in, and unbelievably, the engine started.'

'Where did you drive to?'

'I searched the road, for Felicity and the mysterious car, but couldn't see either. I … I was so scared. My mind went into autopilot, and I drove back to Calvin's flat, but he wasn't there. My ankle throbbed; I was in agony by this point. I could only think of Charing Cross Hospital in Hammersmith; it's not far, so I went there. I thought I could alert somebody about what had happened to us.'

Rocky wrote a note and slide it along the table to Fraser. 'And did you? Alert someone?'

She wiped her eyes clear of tears and nodded. 'I explained to the nurse in A&E what had happened to me and my friend. She contacted the police and someone came and took my statement. He told me to go home and wait. I did … I shouldn't have. It's my fault.'

Hamilton made a quick note to follow up on Holly's alibi, and ensure Clarke questioned Calvin Robinson of his whereabouts once his friends had vacated his home. Now, he needed the pair to press on with Holly. As if Fraser had heard his internal pleas, the line of questioning turned in the direction he wanted.

'Miss Walker, we understand what a difficult time this is for you,' she said, 'but we need your help to capture the person, or persons, who murdered your two friends.'

Holly's head snapped up. 'Of course. I'll do everything I can.'

Fraser smiled. 'I need you to tell us about the last time you saw Donna Moran. What exactly happened at Lake Windermere, and why she disappeared without a word to you, her friends.'

Hamilton watched the colour drain from Holly's face. The twitching and fidgeting stopped, as though the woman froze in time for a few moments. Before breaking through the barrier of the past, she inhaled deeply.

'I don't understand. What has this got to do with Donna?' Holly asked.

'Can you honestly say you *don't* think it has anything to do with your friend, Miss Walker? Considering the date and location of Warren Speed's murder. And now, his fiancée …' Fraser trailed off.

Hamilton liked his colleague's tactic; he knew her words would hang in the air like a thick mist. Holly's eyes darted away. Her head hung low.

'We all thought the same thing … or, at least that it was possible. It's the reason we met last night,' the woman confessed, her hands falling limp in her lap. 'I honestly don't know if Donna is alive. If she's doing this to us. But she'd probably have reason to.'

'Why?' Fraser implored. 'Tell us what happened.'

'It was a stupid, alcohol-induced dare. We'd made our way over to the castle's boat house and continued drinking. The darkness descended around us, and Warren saw the opportunity to play his usual prankster role. He dared one of us to stay in the boat house for the night. Donna, besotted and hanging on to his every word, agreed to do it. But Flick decided to up the ante, and instructed Donna to stay overnight in a rickety dinghy chained up inside the boat house.'

Holly looked away again. A red flush crept along her neck and rested in her round cheeks. She refused to make eye contact while Fraser spoke.

'What did you, Calvin, and Todd think about all this?'

Holly sighed. 'I asked her not to do it. It might have been the summer, but … it had become so cold, so quickly. Calvin didn't like the idea; he's never been a fan of any type of bullying. Suffered enough persecution himself growing up. Warren was hell-bent on the idea, and Donna would never turn him down. She got in the boat, and we left. We all just left her there.'

'But she returned to the B&B you were staying at?' Rocky said and he sat forward in the chair. 'She collected her belongings before returning to London?'

Holly shrugged. 'I never saw her again.'

'I don't understand,' Fraser said, frowning. 'In Felicity's statement, she said Donna had taken her bag and left a note explaining she wanted to get home.'

'We all had our own rooms. It was late when we woke, and Flick assumed Donna would have just returned to the B&B and forgot about the stupid dare, so she went looking for her in her room. That's when she found the note. But … what must have happened to Donna out there to make her up and leave us without a word?'

'Did you all leave Donna at the boat house at the same time?'

Holly puckered her lips and hummed. 'I can't … I'm not sure. I'd had too much to drink. No, wait, Calvin left first. Yes, that's it. The others were taking photographs, and he didn't want to be involved. Myself, Todd, Warren, and Felicity left about ten minutes later.'

'Thank you, Miss Walker, you've been extremely helpful with our investigation,' Fraser said, as Holly's head fell into her hands.

* * *

Calvin Robinson sat upright and appeared more focused than the last time Hamilton had interviewed him. He watched through the one-way glass, observing the eye contact between Robinson and Clarke.

'When Miss Walker returned to your apartment, less than thirty minutes after leaving, you were nowhere to be found. Where did you go, Calvin?'

'To work. I was on the night shift.'

'At a local coffee shop?'

The young man grunted. 'Clever. I work at the coffee shop during the day, and every now and then, my mate hooks me up with a gig at a local bar.'

Clarke leaned back in his chair. 'What kind of gig was this then?'

'Music. It's my passion. I DJ whenever I get the chance to.'

'And the name of the local bar?'

'The Muse. It's right next the London Eye, and I was there until about three a.m., if you want to check it out?'

Hamilton's partner grinned. 'We will, Mr Robinson. Thank you for the permission. Now, I need you to tell us about the night before Donna Moran disappeared from Ambleside.'

Calvin's chest tensed. 'Well, actually, she went missing from London. And it's your guys who told us that, after we'd reported her missing.'

Clarke nodded. 'Yes, but I asked you to tell us about the night before she left Ambleside. You know, when you and your friends were on the lake, having a drink, or two, at the old boat house.'

Hamilton watched the young man's nostrils flare as his hands balled into fists under the table. It was obvious. Calvin quickly realised one of his friends had said too much to the police.

'It was Donna's idea. I think she wanted to try and impress Warren. We could all see he was getting a bit too friendly with Felicity.'

'And Donna didn't approve of their blossoming relationship?'

Calvin shrugged. 'Well, she never said that, but I guess it was obvious. Donna and Warren had fooled around together, and she didn't want to share him. But it was all light-hearted. It's what you do at university.'

'But you were no longer their university friend. How did that make you feel?'

Calvin visibly blanched at the question. 'What's that supposed to mean?'

'Well, here are your five best friends, all fresh with their degrees, and you're sat with them, just a barman. Were you bitter? Jealous of their relationships?'

The man sucked the air between his teeth. 'No.'

'But you were happy to leave Donna there, alone and unprotected?'

'I make my own choices in life. Donna made hers. It was a bit of fun, and she was well up for it. No one made her stay overnight at that boat house. It was stupid, but it was a laugh.'

'And was it still a laugh when her mother had to report her only daughter missing?' Clarke asked, but Calvin refused to look him in the eye. 'Did you and the others leave the boat house together?'

'Honestly, I didn't think Donna would make the night. Assumed she'd be back within the hour when it got too cold, or she got bored. I headed back to the B&B for another few drinks. It was a decent place; they kept the bar open as long as a guest was drinking. The others went back to their rooms. I guess it was about midnight when I finally decided to turn in.'

'And did you see Donna return to her room?'

The young man hesitated. 'No.'

'What do you think happened to her out there to make her run off back to London without saying a word to any of her friends?' Clarke said and stared at the young man.

Calvin glared down at his hands, one index finger drumming on the table. 'I don't know. Maybe she blamed us for not sticking around … for leaving her there. Maybe … she didn't want to speak to us anymore. I don't know, but I never saw or spoke to Donna again.'

Clarke glanced in Hamilton's direction and ended the interview.

* * *

Hamilton observed Todd Bell with interest. His brown, floppy hair fell casually to one side, and he sat away from the table, one foot comfortably resting on his knee. Dixon didn't question him straight away, but flicked through the file of crime scene photographs for a few minutes. Todd's foot idly bounced up and down.

'You don't seem too upset, Mr Bell, for someone who's just lost yet another friend.'

'Sadly, I'm used to dealing with death in my life. I tend not to wear my heart on my sleeve, shall we say.'

'Yes, I know your parents were killed in the 7/7 bombings –'

'Is that what I'm here to discuss?' Todd interrupted.

Dixon pushed the photographs forward in front of Todd, giving him details about both Warren Speed and Felicity Ireland's murder scenes. He glanced at them for only a second before turning away.

'I don't want to see them.'

'Can you tell us where you were when both of your friends met an untimely death?'

Todd pushed the photographs back to Dixon. 'I was with my girlfriend, Mel, the weekend Warren was in Ambleside. You can have her number and address. Then … when Felicity …' He paused and steadied his breathing. 'I left Calvin's apartment before the girls. I was booked to coach under twelves at a local football club. But it was called off ten minutes before I arrived at the venue.'

'So, where did you go?'

'Home. And, yes, I was alone. Mel was working the night shift at the hospital, and she doesn't stay at mine when she's on nights.'

'What's Mel's job at …?'

'Charing Cross Hospital. She's an A&E nurse.'

'And how long have the two of you been together?'

'Nearly six months now. We met at the coffee shop where Calvin works.'

Dixon paused for a few moments. 'And what was your relationship with Felicity Ireland like?'

Todd's jaw tightened, but his gaze never quitted Dixon's. 'She was my friend.'

'Was there anything ever romantic between the two of you?'

His mouth turned down, and he shook his head. 'Not really, no.'

'What about you and Donna, anything there?'

'I'm not in the habit of sleeping with my friends, Detective. Besides, Warren had a history with both Donna and Felicity, and you don't step to your best friend's women.'

'How did you get those cuts on your hand, Mr Bell?'

He looked down and rubbed his thumb across the grazed skin on his knuckles. Although Dixon had veered off course with the line of questioning, Hamilton was pleased of it. During the previous two interviews, it became clear the friends' recollections of Lake Windermere were not entirely matching. But he wondered if Todd could offer them something different.

'I punched a wall.'

'Lose your temper a lot, do you?'

'No, not usually. But I'd made a stupid decision that day and hated myself for it. I lashed out, at myself may I add, and this was my prize.'

'Care to share what bad decision you'd made, Mr Bell?'

Todd grinned, half-heartedly. 'Women troubles.'

'I see. Do you drive, or own a car?'

'No, I never saw the point in learning. Living in London, everywhere is within walking or tube distance. But, Mel drives and sometimes it's nice to get out of the City.'

'Do you travel out of London together a lot? Perhaps you took your girlfriend to Ambleside, maybe thought you could show her the sights of the lakes you visited before with friends?'

Todd snorted a puff of air and shook his head. 'No, Mel and I have never been to Ambleside together.'

Hamilton took a step closer to the glass, his eyes fixed on Todd, and the beads of sweat brimming at the edge of the man's poised and pale face. There was one final question he wanted the answer to, and he desperately needed Dixon to be on his wavelength right now.

She sat forward in her chair. 'Mr Bell, did you have an affair with Felicity?'

'I already told you, no.'

'Were you jealous of Warren and Felicity's relationship?'

'No.' He placed both feet on the floor.

'Did you hang around Calvin's apartment and then follow Felicity in Mel's car?'

'No.' His jaw tightened.

'Did you murder Felicity Ireland?'

'No! I did not!' he yelled, and slammed his fist on the table.

CHAPTER TWENTY-ONE

The last forty-eight hours have shocked me. I feel more alone and confused than ever before. Felicity told me nothing. Her begging squeals caused the anger inside of me to combust. I had considered freeing her, after a bit of torture, of course, you understand. She deserved it. But the drone of her voice: *I haven't done anything wrong. Donna, please stop this. I don't understand.* It drove me wild.

Can you remember a time when someone told you they saw red? The mist descended, and they attacked. "Blah, blah, bloody blah" is what I used to think to that. We all make our own decisions in life. But I understand now. I felt the mist of uncontrollable anger as I whacked her over the skull with the hammer that had been resting against the table in my shed.

It was her own fault. She unleashed the dark beast. The one I do so well to supress on a daily basis. Especially where my friends are concerned. Well, the people I consider my friends, anyway.

Becky, and then Warren, were premeditated. Planned. On both of those nights, I knew they would die; there was no other option for them. They were disloyal. I was prepared to give Felicity a chance. All she had to do was tell the truth about her friends. Instead, she whinged and wined and demanded answers. I'm in control now, stupid fucking bitch.

Why are you doing this?

Please stop hurting me.

I don't understand.

I laughed at her. Even in the face of death, Felicity's arrogant nature shone through. Always wanting things done her way.

Always wanting something from someone else. She never gave me any credit, and that's why she couldn't see that I know everything.

After the spiders, I unleashed the rat. Watched with excitement as it headed straight for Felicity's body. I'd laid a trap in the dank alleyway near my house and waited weeks. The gigantic rodent, with a tale as fat as its hairy body. Its beady, black eyes bulged, and its nose twitched, ravenous for food after being deprived. It had to wait until I had Felicity in place. Okay, maybe it was premediated, because would I have really rescued her from a flesh-eating parasite?

Probably not.

The rat punctured Felicity's hands and arms, its thirst for blood finally being satisfied. Its squeals of delight were deafening in the small wooden outhouse, and for a second, I worried the neighbours might hear. But the botulism paralysis had already kicked in, worked its magic on Felicity's respiratory system, and I could see the fear in her widened eyes. I smiled.

You see, I saw them together. That bastard, yanking Felicity's T-shirt over her pert and pale tits. Their tongues entwined, as Warren's greedy hands wandered all over her perfect body.

I didn't care. Not really. But I knew the effect it would have on all of us.

I was prepared to give Felicity another chance. If she just told me what I needed to know. If she just told me where they'd hidden Donna's body.

CHAPTER TWENTY-TWO

Hamilton strolled into the public house and made a beeline for Billy, who sat in the corner of the pub with two full pints of beer in front of him. The desire to down the contents of the frosted glass overwhelmed Hamilton. Not a vice he'd given in to for many years, but the stress of the day had caught up with him.

Frustratingly, the majority of his day had been spent with DCI Allen, who had been summoned to Scotland Yard for a press conference. As the Senior Investigating Officer on the Warren Speed and Felicity Ireland case, Hamilton's presence was expected by those demanding answers. While away from the office, his team continued to plough through surveillance footage, phone records, and travel history, but the Newcombs still hadn't been located. He dismissed his team from the incident room, instructing them to have an hour break before returning. His watch hit 8 p.m. as he pulled the chair from underneath the wooden table and joined Billy.

'What are you doing here?' he asked.

His old friend snorted. 'What do you mean, mate? We made plans yesterday … that's why you're here too.'

'Well, considering your sister-in-law was murdered last night, I think a knees-up in your local is a little inappropriate. Don't you, *mate*?'

Billy's pupils dilated, and despite the tense silence that fell between them, his eyes never left Hamilton's gaze.

'I … How? I just …'

'What, Billy, what do you want to know? How I found out? I'm a fucking copper, you idiot. I saw you let yourself into Dorinda

Ireland's home, after I'd told her Felicity was brutally tortured and murdered. I contacted the Family Liaison Officer earlier today, and she confirmed Dorinda's partner, William Thorn, also lived at the address. Now you know what I know, care to tell me what the hell you're playing at?' Hamilton pushed the pint of beer to one side, leaving his clenched fist on the table.

Billy's chest rose and fell at rapid speed, but his face remained calm. 'Yes, what you've discovered is correct. But I had to come and see you, regardless of what's happening. Maybe even more so.'

'Stop with the riddles. I don't have time for this. Where were you the night Felicity was murdered.'

His old friend flinched. 'What? I was at your house. You spoke to me, for heaven's sake, Den. Do you really think if anything dodgy was going on, I'd approach you? Don't forget; I came to you before Felicity was murdered.'

'No, you came before her body was found.' Hamilton paused, searching Billy's face, witnessing nothing but sadness. 'Okay, so why? Why now?'

'I've been with Dorinda for three years, and we have a beautiful daughter called Amelia.' Billy glanced away and cleared his throat. 'Anyway, in that time, I've sorted my life out, and I've got a great job helping other people. I want us to be in each other's lives again, Den. I mean, come on. We've been mates forever.'

He straightened up and stared hard at Billy. 'I'll only ask you one more time, why now?'

'What the hell do you mean, why now? I just explained myself, didn't I?'

'No, that was no explanation. It sounds like the last few years of your life have been pretty cushy, but you wanting to be friends again seems to have come right at the same time you could be mixed-up in a bloody murder investigation.'

'Wait a minute. It's not like that.'

'You turned your back on everyone you knew four years ago, without a word, without a reason. I was going through the toughest time of my life, and you up and left. You know, I looked for you, just for a few weeks. I suppose it took my mind off the heartbreak I was suffering. Then, I found out you'd moved back home, with your mum. All fine and dandy. So, I left you there and forgot all about you.'

'Den, you're being unfair. You know I had some issues … I have had since school, and things just … got worse.'

'You were bullied, and I was always there for you back then.'

'It's not always something that leaves you when you finally get out of school, mate. The bullying shaped the person I became. How hard do you think it is for a grown man to say he's being bullied? To say he's depressed, because the big boys picked on him at school.'

'Depression. Are you being serious? You never once mentioned that to me. In fact, you never mentioned anything. You just disappeared from my life without telling me what happened. What kind of a mate is that?'

'This may be hard to believe, but not everything is about you, *Detective Hamilton*. There's me thinking you'd have a bit of empathy considering what happened to Maggie.'

Hamilton flew from his seat, chair crashing to the floor. He stooped over the table, shoving his face inches from Billy's, and gritted his teeth.

'Don't you ever mention my little girl again, *William*.'

'Denis, I'm s–'

'Shut it! You better bloody watch yourself; if you think for one minute you've got a *friend* on the inside, you're mistaken. If I find out you've got anything to do with these murders, I'll happily slap the cuffs on you myself.'

Hamilton marched back through the pub, his fists balled so tightly the whites of his knuckles looked ready to burst through his brown skin. He drank in the cold air the moment he stepped outside and jogged through the car park. In the stillness of the car, his mind whizzed and bounced between the words he and Billy had just exchanged and scenes from their youth.

Billy had been bullied throughout secondary school by a gang of boys who, when they could be bothered to attend classes, always honed in on the skinny lad with the stutter and thick-rimmed glasses. He'd kept it a secret for a long time, but he noticed Billy recoil whenever the bullies were in the vicinity. It wasn't the first time he'd started a fight to protect his friend, and it gave Billy some cooling off time. Hamilton confided in Mrs Thorn, and Billy soon attended speech-therapy classes and the opticians for contact lenses. He became Billy's security, and with Hamilton there, his friend was never harmed. It never occurred to him to ask what happened when he wasn't around.

But, looking back, Hamilton realised it was thanks to Billy that he even considered joining the Metropolitan Police. The sheer injustice his friend faced on a daily basis at school, and him becoming the shelter from that prejudice, had unintentionally placed him on his career path. A stab of remorse pierced his chest as thoughts turned to his daughter. Thinking of the numerous times he'd witnessed Billy being taunted, should he not have identified Maggie's bullying before it was too late? How could he have saved his friend but not his daughter? And the fact Billy had discarded their friendship, was he really the protector he thought he was?

The vibration from his inside pocket removed Hamilton from his internal reflections.

'DI Hamilton.'

'Gov, it's Rocky. I've just got back to the office, and I think you'll want to as well. They've pulled another body from the Thames.'

* * *

Rocky jumped up from his desk the moment Hamilton burst into the office. He hadn't had the chance to give his boss any further details over the phone, as the line went dead as soon as he'd uttered the word Thames. Pleased Hamilton arrived back to the incident room before the rest of the team, Rocky hoped he could share more than one intriguing piece of information with his superior.

'Who is it?' Hamilton demanded. 'Which of the friends have been targeted now?'

'None of them, gov, but the body has been identified as Jason Newcomb.'

'Shit,' Hamilton muttered. 'What else do we know?'

'Quite a bit,' he replied and gestured for Hamilton to follow him to the computer monitor. He pulled up the clips he'd watched just ten minutes previously. 'Thanks to various passers-by filming different aspects of the scene, we know Jason Newcomb stopped his car in the middle of the Albert Bridge, near Battersea Park, climbed the railings, and jumped to his death. It's all over the news and social media already.'

Hamilton nodded. 'Any sign of his car near the Embankment last night, or Claire Newcomb's?'

'Yes, I eventually found Jason's car on Craven Street, just up from The Playhouse Theatre. It's yards from the Embankment, maybe a five-minute walk. But how the hell would he have got Felicity's body from the car to the Thames, without anyone noticing?'

Hamilton rubbed his forefinger and thumb across the dark stubble, which Rocky thought had long grown past his superior's usual tidy length. He could see Hamilton mulling over everything he'd just shared and wanted to step-up his game and be noticed.

'We have to remember, gov, Felicity Ireland was found rather late. That could be a factor in the transportation of her body.'

'London never sleeps, Rocky. If someone hauled a dead body even five minutes down the road, someone would have noticed.'

'But would anyone have given a second glance to someone pushing a wheelchair?' he said, a thrill bubbling in his stomach.

'What are you getting at?' Hamilton asked, the lines on his forehead furrowing deeper.

'An hour before Felicity Ireland's body was found, there was a hooded figure guiding a wheelchair along the Embankment. I lost sight of it, but picked it up again further down at a step entrance, not too far from the pier. Laura Joseph confirmed with

Dixon that Felicity Ireland did have a high concentrate level of botulinum toxin in her system. Passers-by could have mistaken her for a patient, or ill woman, being aided for a stroll along the Thames at night.'

Hamilton clicked his fingers, and the noise sparked a sense of achievement inside Rocky. 'Jason abandoned the body in plain sight. He would have only needed a small window of time when no one was paying any attention, and he slipped the body from the wheelchair into the water. Felicity would have sunk, initially, giving him enough time to get back to the car and disappear. But then what happens the following night? He feels so guilty he decides to top himself?'

'Maybe he thought we were on to him and believed it a better fate than life in prison.'

Hamilton hummed, and Rocky was unsure if it was a sound of agreement, or not. 'I'll get Fraser to try and access Jason Newcomb's phone records. Perhaps we can get an idea of who he was speaking to in the hours leading up to him jumping from the Albert Bridge. If he had a contact at all, that is.'

Rocky saw his opportunity and grabbed it, knowing the rest of his team were due back shortly. 'Speaking of Fraser, gov, I've got something I wanted to show you.'

He continued to explain the reason why he hadn't left the office with the rest of them, and how he'd used the time to delve into a request Hamilton had asked of him a few weeks previously. While making an arrest in Stratford, Fraser had been struck from behind by an unidentified person, momentarily knocking her out.

'I couldn't find anything from the local street CCTV, but I approached a small boutique which I noticed had a south facing camera outside their shop.'

'What did you find, Rocky?'

'Sadly, nothing too conclusive, but I do think it's important, gov,' he said and handed Hamilton a grainy image of Fraser lying on the ground, and a tall man stepping over her.

He tried to read Hamilton's face, but not having worked with his boss long enough, he couldn't tell what was meant when the man arched his right eyebrow, or chewed on his bottom lip. He desperately wanted to add the details about Fraser's drug-addicted friend, but there was no way he'd break her trust.

'I haven't shown this to Fraser yet, gov. I didn't think I should.'

'Yes, you were right to come to me first. It's best not to worry her just yet. And thanks for this. I'll look into it further,' Hamilton agreed, and pocketed the photograph into the inside of his jacket, just as the others entered the office. 'Ah, good, you're all here. We've got some catching up to do and not a lot of time. Let's get to it.'

A wave of exhaustion wrestled with his fleeting moment of achievement, and won. Rocky knew the dark circles under Clarke's eyes mirrored his own, and the tiredness crept through every muscle. But he took strength in Hamilton's speech as he brought the rest of his team up-to-date with the investigation. Working through the night had only ever happened once while stationed at Welwyn Police Station, but he was determined not to allow his inexperience to become a factor. Hamilton had given him a chance by pushing for his promotion to Detective Constable, and he wasn't about to let the team down. Although it was a bonus he'd unearthed a flicker of a clue with the wheelchair, Rocky still believed they were far from the finishing line with this case.

CHAPTER TWENTY-THREE

Despite the late hour, the incident room continued to thrive. With no off-switch for the city of London, the Metropolitan Police never rested either; always an officer somewhere working on an unsolved case. Hamilton glanced over the still CCTV image Rocky had given him earlier, before placing it into the top drawer of his office desk. He wondered if there really was any significance it in, but didn't want to dismiss the new recruit's eagerness, and promised to give it his dedicated time, when they solved their current perplexing case.

Hamilton read the case files repeatedly, until the black letters on the white pages began to merge together. Adamant he was missing something, he swigged the dregs of his cold cup of tea and rummaged through the statements for the umpteenth time. Although Warren Speed had been in the public eye, Hamilton dismissed the murderer as being a stalker fan due to the connection with Donna Moran and the lure to Ambleside. With a heavy head, as the same names and evidence swirled through his mind, Rocky's knock on the door was a welcome break.

'Gov, thought I'd let you know, Fraser managed to get hold of Jason Newcomb's phone records,' the young lad said from the doorway. 'He called two numbers before he jumped from the Albert Bridge, an untraceable number and his sister, Claire.'

He sighed. 'We need to find that woman. Any updates or sightings?'

Rocky shook his head. 'Sorry, gov.'

Hamilton's eyes wandered over the mountains of paper on his desk, before addressing Rocky again. 'Work with Clarke and Dixon. I want you to revisit Claire Newcomb's home and see if she's hiding out there. She may think that, at this late hour, no-one will come knocking. Also, touch base with Mel King; we've not interviewed her yet, but she's Todd Bell's girlfriend and works at the hospital. These people seem so twisted together. Dixon could be right about the crime of passion.'

He stopped briefly to grab a pen and sheet of paper from his desk and jotted a name down, before handing the paper to Rocky.

'What's this, gov?'

'Nothing at the moment. But pass that on to Fraser and ask her for a background check. Tell her to report back to me immediately.'

'Sure thing. Where will you be?'

'I'll be here. Something's caught my attention on these background files, and I need to make a few calls,' Hamilton replied and waited for Rocky to leave before lifting the receiver and dialling his mother's home phone number.

Once Philippa had calmed down, shocked by her son's call so close to midnight, she asked why he'd phoned.

'I'm working on a case, and one of the people we've interviewed has connections with someone in the Lake District. She's an elderly lady, living in Keswick. It's a long shot, I know, but I wondered if you might know her?'

Philippa sniggered. 'And you're asking me because all old women know each other?'

'Mum –'

'Ha! What's the woman's name then, or do I have to guess it?'

'Monica Summers.'

Hamilton winced, pulling the phone away at the sound of his mother's shrieking laughter growing louder and louder.

'Would you Adam and Eve it, I do bloody know the woman,' she said, once the giggles had subsided. 'What do you need to know, love?'

He raised his eyebrows, a slight sigh escaping through his pouted lips; he hadn't really expected his mother to be of any help.

'Well, what can you tell me about her?'

Philippa's muffled moans and groans travelled down the line, and Hamilton envisioned his mother making herself comfortable. He'd never call her a gossip, but she was usually the first to know what happened on their street when he was growing up.

'She's a lovely lady, Denis. We hold a book club meeting in my tea room once a month, and she always makes the journey from Keswick to attend. It's not a million miles away, I know, but she's old and very frail. Anyhow, I felt bad one evening, and so I offered to drive her home after the book club. She told me all about her husband; he was been a doctor, but passed away some years ago, and they could never have kids. They fostered and adopted for a while. She was here last week, actually, delighted the sale of her house had finally gone through. It had been on the market for over a year.'

'Monica lives alone then?'

'Yes, sad, isn't it? Oh, but the house, love, you should see it.' Philippa whistled. 'It's three-storeys high, up on the hill, with glorious views of the lake. Just amazing. Not that the poor cow gets to appreciate it, says she hasn't been upstairs for about five years. Can you believe that? What a waste. I think she wants to move into a residential care home, the arthritis is too painful now, God love her.'

Hamilton's mother continued to chatter on about Monica Summers and the tea rooms and the latest book the club had chosen to read. Despite the phone resting against his ear, his mind ran away with his thoughts.

'Mum, has she ever mentioned any of the children she'd adopted? Do any of them still visit?'

Philippa grunted, clearly not found of being interrupted mid-flow. 'No, they bloody well don't visit. Isn't that gratitude for you? The two adopted daughters left for university three or four years ago, and haven't visited since, she told me. Although, one of them does write regularly throughout the year, checking on Monica's health, and if she still lives in that grand house all alone. I guess that's better than nothing, hey?'

'Yeah. Look, Mum, I'm going to pass Mrs Summers' details on to a colleague local to the area, so someone from the constabulary might pop in to visit her. Purely routine, nothing of significance, but don't be telling everyone at your book club, okay?'

'Don't be silly, son, what do you take me for?'

His attention was distracted by Fraser, who now stood in the office doorway, waving the same piece of paper he'd written on not twenty minutes earlier. Hamilton said goodbye to his mother, promising to call her for an unrelated work chat soon.

'Come in, Fraser. I'm sorry to be bombarding you with things, but I've made a few notes, and I need you to get in touch with Inspector Bennett's office in Cumbria.'

'No problem, I can add that to my list. Now, about the name you gave me; I wasn't exactly sure what it was you wanted me to find out,' Fraser said and took a seat opposite Hamilton. 'But after a quick search I discovered William Thorn has lived with Dorinda Ireland, a self-employed landscape gardener, for three years. But what I think you'll be interested in is Mr Thorn works at Brunel University, and has done so for the last three years, as a student counsellor. I assumed that could be the link you were looking for –'

Hamilton jumped from his chair and marched into the incident room, his eyes darting around until they landed on one of his team.

'Good, you're still here, Dixon. Come on, you're with me,' he growled.

Fraser rushed up behind him. 'Boss, who's this Thorn guy?'

Hamilton attempted to control his unsteady breathing and calm his erratic heart rate. He unclenched his fists and thrust his hands into his trouser pockets, while looking between the two female sergeants either side of him, both waiting for answers. With a heaviness in his voice, Hamilton explained his connection to Billy, or William as he was more commonly known now, and the discovery of his old friend's relationship with the victims and university.

'So, you want to go and have a word with him now?' Dixon questioned, her usually wide eyes now small and red.

'Of course I do, regardless of the time. I want to know why my old school friend is trying to push himself back into my life, and exactly what it is he's hiding. Fraser, concentrate on the last four years and see what else you can find out about Billy; where he's lived, and worked, who he's socialised and interacted with.'

Hamilton broke off and stared aimlessly into the office. The anger swam through him like hot lava as he pictured his oldest mate lying and deceiving him. However, he wasn't about to lose the momentum with this case, and he tried to shake off the irritation gnawing at his skin.

'Boss, it can be difficult to talk to a friend in these circumstances. Would you prefer if I attended with Dixon?' Fraser asked, her tone light but forceful.

'I'll be fine; William Thorn hasn't been a friend of mine for some time now. Right, Dixon, let's get on with this.'

* * *

Hamilton thumped on the front door harder than necessary, disturbing the quietness of a sleepy street after 1 a.m. He eyed Dixon, but she looked away. Pulling his shoulders tall, he inhaled deeply through his nose and fixed his suit jacket back into place. There was no way he wasn't getting the opportunity to talk to Billy first.

The door opened, and Hamilton was surprised to find his old friend fully clothed and looking wide awake. The pair glared at each other, their breathing synced as unspoken words and questions passed between them, until Dixon cleared her throat and broke the spell off.

'I guess you should come in,' Billy said and opened the door further, before walking to the back of the house.

The steam from the kettle whistled as Hamilton and Dixon entered the kitchen. The stench of coffee filled the room, and the humming laptop on the dining table showed signs of life.

What Hamilton wanted to know was, had his old friend been sat waiting for him to knock on the door?

'Dorinda's staying with a close family friend tonight, and I always find it hard to sleep when she's not here,' Billy said, while filling three mugs with hot water. 'I'm always worried I won't hear Amelia if she wakes in the night. I've been using the time to get some work done.'

Hamilton pulled a metal chair away from the table and sat down. 'University work?'

Billy exhaled loudly, dropped the teaspoon to the work surface, and turned to face the detectives. 'I wondered how long that would take.'

'What? For us to find out you actually have more than one connection with two murder victims? You should have saved us all some time and told me yourself.'

'Which I would have done, if you weren't so bloody suspicious the last time I spoke to you.'

He chortled. 'Really, Billy? Well, why don't you make things easier for yourself now and tell me exactly where you were the night Felicity Ireland was murdered.'

Billy moved slowly, sliding a mug along the breakfast island to Dixon, who had refused to take a seat but held her notebook and pen in hand. He then deposited the other two cups on the table and pulled out the chair opposite Hamilton. He blew over the hot contents of the mug before sipping, eyes remaining fixed on Hamilton over the rim.

'If you're calling me a murderer, I don't know what kind of friend you are, Den,' Billy eventually spoke, and lowered the mug onto the table.

'I'm Detective Inspector Hamilton, Mr Thorn, not your friend. My question is a serious one, and if you have a problem answering it, we can have this conversation at the station.'

Hamilton's body tensed, shocked by Billy's demeanour; it was curious for his friend to be so confident and cocky. The coffee aroma wafted up from the mug into his nostrils, and he pushed it away. They might not have spoken for four years, but Billy knew of Hamilton's disgust for the beverage.

'Come on, there's no need for all this, Den. We're bloody mates, and I'll tell you anything you want to know, no bother.'

'I've already asked you –'

'Yes, yes, okay. That night, I finished worked at about 5 p.m., I locked the office door, left the building, and got into my car. I drove to The Duck in the Pond pub, had one pint, and then drove round to your house. I waited outside for a while, I don't know, maybe half an hour. I saw Elizabeth come home, but thought it best I waited for you. After you drove off like a bat out of hell, I went back to the pub. Left the car there, and by the time I'd walked home, Dorinda had been told the news about Felicity.'

'Did you know Felicity before you started working at Brunel University?'

'No. And I met Dorinda through Felicity one evening at the bar.'

'A habit of yours to socialise with your students?'

'It's not like that, Den. They're not my *students*, like you think. I'm not there to teach them; they're not sent to me if they don't hand in coursework, or anything like that.'

Hamilton shrugged and turned down his lips. 'Do explain your role to us then.'

'A friend of mine is an influential player on the faculty board at the university. A few years ago, he heard I was having a tough time and was out of work. He'd wanted to run an experiment at Brunel, create a place where the students could go if they needed some counselling, advice, or just someone to talk to. My office may be located on campus, and I may be paid by the university, but I'm seen as a separate entity. A place for students to feel safe.'

'Hmm … I'd still bet it's not a great idea for you to drink with said students. So, was it a regular occurrence?'

Billy sighed, and Hamilton saw the resolve fade from his eyes; now, he looked tired. 'It was a one off, a university celebration, many of the facility were there. Felicity introduced me to Dorinda, but nothing happened straight away. A few weeks later, I bumped into her in Uxbridge, and we went for a coffee. I'm sure you're not so straight-laced these days I have to explain how things progressed from there.'

'What about Felicity's friends, and partner, Warren Speed? How well did you know them?'

'Well, Warren was Felicity's fiancé; he was like family to me and Dorinda. But we didn't really socialise with them. There was one friend, Calvin, I saw him on campus quite a lot, and we chatted a few times.'

'About what?' Hamilton probed.

'Nothing in particular, really. He was a cool kid and served me lunch in the bar sometimes. He said his grades weren't good enough to join his friends in lectures, but I liked him. Actually, he reminded me of you a little bit. Blessed with street smarts and the gift of the gab.'

Dixon laughed from behind Hamilton, and he rolled his eyes. 'Chatty is not how I'd describe myself, Billy,' he retorted.

It was Billy's turn to snigger. 'No, you look a bit uptight these days, I must admit. But you certainly *used* to be the life and soul of every party, Den.'

Hamilton thought of how much his life had changed since the days of being a free-spirited eighteen-year-old. The recollections didn't feel like his own any more. Could he really have been that young lad? Afro-hair grown longer than his mother approved of, partying until the small hours of the morning, and caring for no one but himself. The memories danced out of his reach, like the wisps of a dandelion he couldn't catch. By twenty-one, he'd married, become a father, busy tying the cravat of his police uniform, and preparing for years of staring death in the face, including in his own home. But he knew now was not the time to think of Maggie.

'I'm not the only one who's changed,' he finally replied, as he eyed Billy, a figure from his past he also didn't recognise.

'Yeah, well, sometimes, life deals you a shitty hand …' Billy paused and sighed. 'I'm sorry, Den, I know you've had your fair share of –'

'Leave it,' Hamilton interrupted. Although stunned his old friend's thoughts had gone to the same place as his own, it was a conversation he wasn't ready to have with Billy, and decided to press on with his questions. 'Did you ever speak with Donna Moran, another friend of both Felicity and Warren's, who attended Brunel with them?'

The colour drained from Billy's face, and as he mumbled incoherently, his eyes fluttering between Hamilton and Dixon. He repeated the question, propelled by the hope of not being lied to. But could he read Billy as easily as when they were friends? Hamilton wondered. He noticed Dixon lift her head and study the man in front of them.

'I met her a few times.' Billy paused to lick his dry lips. 'On campus, she visited my office once to talk about her coursework; although her grades were good, it was something she continually worried about, which could lead to panic attacks sometimes.'

'And the other times?'

Billy rubbed his hand back and forth over his cropped, dark hair. 'Erm … at Felicity's house. She was having a BBQ, and I dropped Dorinda round, popped in briefly to say hi. Then, at their graduation ceremony, before …'

'Before Donna Moran went missing,' Hamilton finished Billy's sentence and sat forward, resting his arms on the table. 'Did you see, or speak, to Donna Moran after their trip to Ambleside?'

Billy shook his head, but wouldn't meet Hamilton's gaze. 'I helped distribute flyers and posters around campus after her disappearance. Felicity was in a bad place, really struggling to understand why her friend had run away. Dorinda hadn't long given birth to Amelia, so I tried to help them both out as best I could.'

Dixon took a step towards the table and hovered over both men. 'Mr Thorn, were you having an affair with Felicity?'

'What?' Billy exclaimed. 'Don't be ridiculous. Dorinda and I may not be married, but I still thought of her sister as my own.'

'We have to ask these questions, you understand, Mr Thorn,' Dixon said.

Hamilton rose and stood next to his colleague. 'We may need you to come down to the station to make an official statement,' he informed Billy. 'And we may have some more questions for you as the case develops.'

'Of course, whatever you need. You know where I am now.'

As Dixon left the room, Hamilton glanced back at his old friend, the man he barely recognised. He wondered if the unfamiliarity was due to how much Billy had changed, or in fact, how much he himself had changed in the past four years.

CHAPTER TWENTY-FOUR

The police are complete fucking idiots. They chase around and around for days, weeks, and months, even bloody years, in some cases, and are they any the wiser? I wonder if they actually know what they're doing, or if it's all a game of luck for them. If they catch a piece of CCTV, or if a witness gives them information, or if they find DNA at a crime scene. It's what they wait for. They are handed all these little shreds of clues, and sometimes it works, I guess, but other times people are left to take the law into their own hands. So, I can totally understand why the number of criminals continues to increase year after year. And why more and more people choose to join a gang … a family of protection. The police can't help you.

I must be crazy, because part of me wants them to know it's me. I'm the one clearing up their fucking mess and finding out the truth, finding out what really happened to Donna. She was abandoned by her friends, ignored by the police, and I won't rest until everyone involved has paid for it. They had a chance to help her but decided to do nothing.

Donna reminded me so much of Becky. Exquisite to watch. The blinding sun bounced off them, glimmering against the golden strands of their hair, and tracing their milky skin … oh, so soft to touch. But as beautiful as they were, they were weak. I tried to save them both, but it was too late; they'd been misled. They were used by the very people they trusted, by the ones they thought loved them.

I loved them.

They belong to me. Even in death.

I've spent too many years of my life watching people have what I can't. Why wasn't I entitled to loving parents, who would beam with pride as I walked onto the stage and accepted a university degree? A mother to read me bedtime stories, and a father to take me out for my first legal drink. Why wasn't I wrapped in the security blanket of older brothers and sisters, there to always fight my corner, no matter what? Or enjoy the fun and squabbles from younger siblings, who I could have taught and guided. To feel the touch of a lover, so genuine and sincere I'd only need look in their eyes to know I was the most important thing in their life.

Instead, I had selfishness forced upon me. I've never found it easy to share things. Or people, for that matter. For that, I blame my parents, who decided to bring me into this cruel world as an only child. When other adults in my life finally expected me to share, it was too late. I'd become the person I was destined to be. Over time, that selfishness transformed into self-interest, and it grew inside me like a tumour. Except, I enjoy my own cancer. I take pleasure in having what I desire the most. We were poor, and childhood wasn't the best experience for me. While kids ran loose on their bikes and scooters, and had holidays aboard, I watched from the side-lines with nothing. The age of innocence, snatched from me because this city is evil and unfair. So, now I have the power to, I'll take everything I want … no matter the consequences. Because who's ever cared about me?

It's time for Donna to join Becky. The two women who helped shape me, loved me like I needed to be – like I deserved to be – but who ultimately betrayed me in the end. They'll be together in death.

Now, you understand why no one is safe.

I will find Donna, dead or alive, and God help anyone who gets in my way.

CHAPTER TWENTY-FIVE

After a few hours rest, and a toasted cheese sandwich, Hamilton drove back to Charing Cross Station just as the sun began to rise over the iconic buildings of London. He hoped the rest of the team had managed to indulge in more sleep than he had. After restlessly tossing and turning in bed for over half an hour, he took solace on the sofa, so as not to wake his wife.

He felt the answers of this case were in his grasp, but the truth continued to evade him. After a quick phone call to Clarke, he ascertained they were still no closer to finding Claire Newcomb, as her flat remained in darkness. While Mel King had clocked off from her late shift at the hospital, his partner and Rocky were unable to locate the woman at home. As he filled his stomach with the warm delights, knowing it was probably the only chance he'd get to eat all day, he conducted a plan of action for the team.

Frustrated by the amount of elusive characters, unclear background information, and unanswered questions, he began the day with a new determination. A surge of energy soared through his body, as his internal self demanded a clear motive and suspect for these crimes.

'Today, we focus on Claire and Jason Newcomb,' he explained to the team, once they had all assembled in the incident room.

'Boss, toxicology report on Jason came back this morning,' Fraser called out. 'It shows high levels of alcohol and cocaine present in his system. Even if the coast guard had arrived sooner and dragged him out of the water, it's unlikely he would have survived the fall from the bridge.'

Hamilton folded his arms and frowned. 'Felicity Ireland's body was disposed of in an inconspicuous manner. It was planned, precise, and careful. These are not the words I'd use to describe Jason Newcomb, from what I've heard of him so far.'

'The drugs and alcohol could have been used purely out of fear, boss. They may not have been substances he used on a regular basis.'

'Well, this is the information I expect you to supply me with, Fraser,' Hamilton bellowed, just as the office phone shrilled over him. 'We should already bloody know if narcotics are a habit for Jason Newcomb.'

'Gov, we've got some more information about the last call Jason Newcomb made to his sister, Claire,' Clarke announced, and hung up the telephone. 'He left a voicemail apologising for everything he'd done and urged her to remain safe.'

Hamilton thought over the message and contemplated the idea that they had been accomplices in the Speed and Ireland murders. Infatuation, love, or lust could have been triggers to end the relationship between Warren and Felicity, allowing the pair to swoop in and rescue them. Yet, he thought, the remorse and guilt shown by Jason's suicide could point to the tragic deaths not being part of the plan; rage and passion infused at some stage in the timeline. Warning his sister to stay safe urged Hamilton on; the need to find the woman more imperative than ever before. He rubbed his thumb and forefinger along the days-old chin stubble.

'Dixon, you're with me,' he said, snapping to attention. 'While we're out, I want the rest of you to find any and every link the Newcomb's had with Warren Speed, Felicity Ireland, and Donna Moran.'

Hamilton marched from the office, Dixon trailing behind as she grabbed her handbag and jacket. He let his thoughts simmer, hoping his assumptions were correct, while making his way to the car parked on Agar Street outside the station.

'Where are we going, boss?' Dixon enquired, as he manoeuvred out into the bustling town.

'Claire Newcomb's home address.'

'Again? Are we going to search the property?'

'We might not need to, Dixon.' He puckered his lips and waited a few minutes before speaking again. 'We're bound to hit some traffic this early in the morning. Why don't you tell me a little bit more about you and your family? Sometimes, I feel like the car is the only place I can get to know new members of my team.' Hamilton glanced over and noticed the pink flush tingeing her sun-kissed cheeks. 'If you don't mind. Of course, we could just listen to the radio?'

She smiled at his light-hearted tone. 'Erm … okay. What about me? As you know, I've been married to Warren for ten years, and we have two children. Sabrina is nine, and Ali is seven. We live in Amersham now, which is lovely, but I've lived all over the UK since I was two.'

'You were born in Morocco, right?' he said, remembering the brief conversation Dixon had had with his wife when they first met at his home.

'Yes, Marrakesh.'

'Do you visit often?'

Dixon groaned. 'My mother's family frowned on her relationship with my father, he's only five years older than her, but they met when she was a teenager. The city became a trendy place in the seventies, and with the tourism came western musicians, artists, fashion, and models. Huge investments were made in Marrakesh, and it began to flourish and develop. Sadly, my maternal grandparents did not, and when they discovered their only daughter was pregnant, out of wed-lock, to a British singer in a band, they were infuriated.'

'Anyone I might know … your father, I mean?'

She smiled. 'No, a small-time band really, but he left them when my mother fell pregnant, wanted to do right by her. They tried to live in Marrakesh, but my grandparents never accepted him. So, we moved to his home town of London, and he became a tour manager. He succeeded in living out his musical dream, in some form or another.'

'It can be hard when families fall apart, but we shouldn't take for granted the time we have with them. After all, you can't choose your family, Dixon.'

'No, but sometimes blood isn't thicker than water,' she said, with a shrug.

Hamilton drummed his fingers on the steering wheel as he contemplated her words and briefly thought of his own father, and the abandonment he'd faced as a young teenager. Hell-bent on never succumbing to emotional outbursts where his father was concerned, he pushed away the image of the man and focused on the case. He wondered now, if they could locate Claire Newcomb, would she show loyalty to her brother? Or was there a glimmer of hope she'd be the key to unlocking some of their unanswered questions?

Outside the woman's home, Hamilton surveyed the building and instructed Dixon to prepare for a chase, signalling to the side entrance of the semi-detached house with two fingers. She nodded in acknowledgment and stood a few feet from the door. He lingered over the two doorbells for a few moments, before pressing 1A. The echo of the buzzer rang out while he refused to budge his finger.

'Alright, alright!' a voice came from behind the communal front door. 'What's going on?'

'Mr Nelson, you may remember me.'

'Yes, of course I do. I told you everything I know about Claire. Why are you harassing me?' the man grumbled.

'It's hardly harassment, sir. But it is extremely important we speak with Miss Newcomb. About her brother.'

Mr Nelson's large frame blocked the view behind the doorway, his hand tightly gripping onto the door, and he lowered his head.

'I know you're hiding Claire,' Hamilton said.

The man shook his head and looked up. Sighing heavily, he peered over his shoulder and shouted, 'She's not here, Detective.'

Hamilton gestured with his fingers again, and Dixon ran around the side of the house. He stepped forward, preparing to knock against the door to gain entry. But Mr Nelson simply stood back, holding the door open for him. The man's cheeks flushed and he looked away, as Hamilton stormed through the unsuccessful bouncer.

He glanced up the stairs, in the direction of Claire's apartment, but was distracted by a thump behind the open front door to his right. He ran into Mr Nelson's apartment. Caught off guard, Hamilton gasped at the sound of a door slamming shut and glass smashing onto the floor. Running along the hallway to the back of the flat, Hamilton's shoes crunched the broken shards of glass as he pulled open the backdoor. Greeted by high-pitched screams, he watched Dixon tackle Claire Newcomb off the fence and drag her onto the lawn.

He raised his eyebrows. 'Well, everything certainly looks like it's under control here.'

'It sure is, boss,' Dixon shouted, as she straddled the suspect and pinned her down in place.

The woman was wearing the classic, white Converse he'd seen her in at Lake Windermere, though the recent wall climbing and grass wrestling had subdued their white glow. Claire's attire was more casual; faded jeans and a black T-shirt, but her poker-straight blonde hair flew in the wind as she thrashed her head and body under the petite, but powerful, Sergeant. From first impressions, Hamilton thought Dixon had captured a wild animal, a woman who obviously had something to hide. But as he walked closer, and Claire began to calm down, he saw the look of sheer panic in her eyes.

'You have to help me,' she yelled, her face flattened to the leafy ground. 'I'm in danger. My life is in danger.'

Dixon handcuffed Claire's wrists behind her back, and as she stood from her kneeling position, dragged the captured woman up with her.

'Miss Newcomb, you're in a lot of trouble,' Hamilton said, and they walked back towards the broken door. Mr Nelson stood in the kitchen, one hand over his pale forehead. A tad dramatic,

Hamilton thought. 'So are you, considering I believe Miss Newcomb's been hiding out here the entire time.'

Mr Nelson dropped his hand and sighed. 'How? How did you know?'

'We haven't been able to find your car anywhere, Miss Newcomb,' Hamilton said and turned back to face the male neighbour. 'After my officers visited again last night, I asked if your blue Ford was still outside. I found it strange you chose to park a decent looking car on the main street, in not the best of neighbourhoods, let's be frank, when you have what looks like a perfectly good garage attached to your apartment. Why would anyone do that, Mr Nelson?

The man stumbled over his own words. 'I … Erm … use it for garden equipment.'

'So, if we were to open it now, we wouldn't find Miss Newcomb's Mini Cooper inside?'

'You can't do that without a warrant.'

Hamilton shrugged. 'No? Well, in all fairness, I couldn't care less right now. After Claire's brother warned her to stay hidden, I had an inkling she was closer to home than we'd imagined. You obstructed my investigation, and you're not off the hook for that, but we've got the woman we came for, and that takes priority. I'll be back for a chat about your involvement in all this, Mr Nelson.'

'Please, stop!' Claire yelled, shaking the fallen strands of hair from her face. 'It's not Roger's fault. He was trying to help me. He wanted me to come and talk to you.'

'That may be so, Miss Newcomb, but we've been trying to locate you for some time now, and Mr Nelson hindered that. It's a criminal offence.'

Tears fell silently down Claire's face. 'I know about my brother. I know about the murders, and I can explain everything. But, please, don't punish Roger for my mistakes. I'll tell you everything you need to know. You just have to keep me safe.'

Hamilton's gaze flickered between Mr Nelson and Claire. Pain and apprehension were etched in the lines on their faces and in the tautness of their mouths. A secret had been shared between them and, despite the obvious reluctance to divulge it, its desire to break free was as strong as a caged bird. The need to finally sing her song of turmoil was evident in the woman's pleading eyes.

'You've got yourself a deal, Miss Newcomb.'

Refusing to wait any longer for a confession, Hamilton insisted on conducting the interview with Claire right there and then in Mr Nelson's living room. Of course, he knew more work would be needed in the aftermath to ensure the statement met official procedures, but the eagerness running through his body made him tremble. However, the quivering blonde managed to pull back some fight, and point blank rejected Hamilton's immediate interview. The woman would tell all, but only in the safety of a police station. With clenched fists, but perhaps also a glimpse of understanding, he led Claire Newcomb from her hideout.

Half an hour later, in an interviewing room at Charing Cross, Hamilton's left foot danced instinctively on the tiles, and he crossed his arms, tucking his hands under his armpits; anything to stop further impatient jittering. While Dixon prepared the recording equipment, Claire sat opposite him, wringing her hands together.

'Firstly, you have to understand, I didn't know what my brother was doing,' Claire said, after she'd been invited to speak by Dixon. 'If I did, I would have stopped him, or called the police myself.'

'When did you find out?' Hamilton asked, his tense body never relaxing.

'When I called him from Lake Windermere … after I'd spoken to you by the old boat house, he already knew Warren was dead. I was overwhelmed with panic. And fear. I didn't know what to do. I left … came home to meet Jason. He confessed everything to me, and even made me feel like my own life was in danger. You see, it wasn't the plan for me to travel to Ambleside with Warren; he was supposed to be on his own. So, by that point, I knew too much. I had to hide. Roger found me having a full-on panic attack in the communal hallway.'

'So, why did your brother kill Warren? And was he also involved with Felicity Ireland's murder?'

Claire frowned. 'Jason didn't kill anyone. Well, not exactly. But the person he's been seeing … that's who's responsible for both Warren and Felicity's murder. That's why he took his own life. The guilt, it got too much for him. When he realised he was being used … for his car, for the vials he could steal from work … for everything … The guilt must have eaten away at him. I never thought it was something he'd do, but … He knew he'd be arrested for all those crimes too.'

Dixon slid a box of tissues across the table, and the woman accepted a handful to wipe her tearful eyes. Hamilton sat forward; a spark ignited in his stomach.

'Claire, who was your brother involved with?'

She looked away, a red flush radiated on her cheeks. 'Am I safe? I need assurance that my life is safe. But also, I can't be arrested for anything to do with this. I only found out last week, and I … I've been …'

'Confused and scared,' Hamilton said softly, and held eye contact with the shaken woman. 'We completely understand. Tell us who was manipulating Jason, and we'll do everything we can to keep you safe.'

Claire looked him straight in the eyes and whispered, 'Holly … Holly Walker.'

CHAPTER TWENTY-SIX

Six months ago

Felicity stood on the corner of the street, the cold February wind clawing at her skin until every inch of her face became numb. Her body begged her to move on, uncertain why she was allowing the tips of her toes to freeze, despite the initial warmth from the fleece-lined Ugg boots. But she'd been compelled to come. On autopilot, she made the journey on public transport, in the opposite direction of her home, to stand outside The Winner's Gym. She couldn't even be sure the person she wanted to see would be in there.

After half an hour of waiting, and just as Felicity's shaking body was about to leave, she saw her friend step out of the gym. Holly's long, dark hair was pulled into a tight bun at the top of her head, odd strands framing her flushed face. The glimmer of sweat surfaced around her make-up free features. Despite Holly looking at home in the cropped leggings and sports footwear, Felicity couldn't see any sign of a trimmer figure on her friend.

'Well, well, well,' Holly said, clocking her straight away. 'What are you doing hanging around on street corners after six o'clock? You'll get a name for yourself like that.'

Felicity smiled at her old friend's instant sarcasm. 'Freezing my tits off. If I waited any longer for you, my nipples could cut glass.'

'Interesting image.' Holly raised her eyebrows and glanced along the street.

'I'm alone. I just thought …' She sighed and rubbed her hands together. 'Do you think we could get a cup of coffee, before I really do become an ice sculpture for the tourists to photograph?'

The nearest café, one the two friends had visited regularly before Donna's disappearance, was situated on the next street. Felicity and Donna would often meet Holly after one of the many classes or work-out routines she took part in since joining the gym at the beginning of term. Finally, when the heat of the small, but busy, café began to warm Felicity, she slipped off her coat, but wrapped her fingers around the hot mug.

'You're looking well. Can't believe you're still going to that gym.'

Holly grunted. 'Why, because I'm still as heavy as ever, so it's hardly doing me any favours?'

'No. I didn't mean that … you're not fat. Or heavy. I just meant …'

'It's fine. You know me, I am what I am. And in the words of Kenny from South Park, I'm not fat, I'm big boned.' The two women laughed together. 'I figure I might as well turn what I do have into muscle, or try at least. It was a kick-boxing class this evening.'

Felicity nodded, slouching in the chair slightly and bringing the cup closer to her face. 'Well, it's paying off. Like I said, you look great.'

Holly rolled her eyes and stared out the window at the crowd of people rushing by after a hard day's work. Felicity watched her friend, now suddenly wishing she was at home, snuggled-up on the sofa with Warren.

'So, come on, Flick. What's this all about? I haven't seen you for nearly a year, and now you're hanging about the gym waiting for me, like old times.'

She hesitated, sitting up in her chair and resting her elbows on the grey table. 'I don't know … just wanted to see a familiar face, I guess.'

'Does Warren know you're here? Because you haven't wanted to see this face for a long time. Nor has he. I've made my peace with it. Shit happens in all friendships.'

Felicity's head dipped to the side as she looked into Holly's sad eyes. A jolt of guilt stabbed her in the chest, and she reached across to hold her friend's hand.

'Warren proposed at the weekend, Hols. I'm so excited, but I just couldn't shout about it to the world until I'd told you first. I'm not even sure why, but …'

Holly snatched her hand away, causing spits of hot coffee to splatter onto Felicity's skin. She reached for a napkin to wipe herself, but when she looked back at Holly, the sadness in her friend's eyes had disappeared. They'd become darker and smaller, and an evil snarl tugged at her lips.

'What is it?' Felicity asked. 'I thought you'd be pleased for us both. We all decided we needed to move on, and that's exactly what the two of us are doing.'

The frown lines deepened in Holly's brow, and she sat forward. Inches from Felicity's face, she spoke under her breath, 'Of course you two are pleasing yourselves, that's all you've ever done.' Spittle flew from her mouth. 'It suited you both to have Donna out of the way, and the two of you made the decision for all of us.'

'No, you're wrong. Donna meant so much to me.'

'You're lying. You just wanted to be with Warren, and with her gone, who would get in your way? Do you know I've never stopped looking for her? I'm always checking Facebook and –'

'Me too, Hols!' Felicity shrieked. 'Whenever possible, I use new contacts to see if they can help me find her, but I've never had any luck. I love Warren, but I never wanted anything bad to happen to Donna. She was my friend. Our friend.'

The creases on Holly's forehead relaxed, but Felicity knew the anger remained beneath the quietness of her friend. She was right, the decision to stop talking to their university friends had been Warren's, but Felicity understood why it needed to happen. Shackling Donna to the old boat house at Lake Windermere, and then leaving her alone, was unforgivable. The fact that none of them had seen her since was life-changing. Warren never forgave himself, and it was too painful to see everyone else.

'Listen, Hols, I deserve to be happy. We all made a decision that night –'

'Hey, I thought it was you,' a timid voice from above interrupted.

Felicity looked up to find a man with greasy, dark hair and blemished skin hovering over them. She was briefly drawn to the small, white scarred tissue of his cheeks and tried to place his face. His blue eyes were friendly and smiling, but the longer she took to recognise him, the more his shoulders slumped.

'I'm so-sorry, I sh-shouldn't have disturbed you,' he stuttered.

Felicity's mobile vibrated on the table, and she looked down to read a message from Warren, demanding to know why she wasn't home yet and who she was with.

'Jason!' she exclaimed as she stood, slipping her phone into her pocket and grabbing her coat.

His beamed. 'Yes. Yes, you remember. I just finished work. It's only down the road, you might know it, The Skin Clinic? It's quite a well-known company. Anyway, I like to pop in here and have a warm cuppa, let the hustle and bustle on the trains die down, before I make my way home. What are you doing here?'

Felicity peered down at Holly, who glared back, her top teeth clamped down on her lower lip. It was all she needed to see to realise it had been a mistake thinking she could share her good news with an old friend.

'I have to go, Holly, I really hope we can catch up again soon.' As Jason shuffled backwards out of her way, Felicity paused. 'I'm sorry I can't stick around, but please, take my seat. I'm sure my friend could do with better company than I've been this evening.'

Felicity ran from the warmth of the café and back outside into the icy elements without another thought for the two people she'd just introduced.

CHAPTER TWENTY-SEVEN

Hamilton abandoned the interview, leaving Dixon and the uniformed officer to finish the interview with Claire Newcomb. He raced into the incident room and demanded one of his team find Holly Walker's address and work details immediately. He then turned to Fraser, beads of sweat beginning to drip from his forehead.

'Did you speak to Inspector Bennett? Get him on the phone this instance.'

'I passed on your notes as requested, boss. I'll call his office now,' Fraser replied as she thumbed through the mountains of files on her desk.

'Gov, Holly Walker works from home,' Clarke said and ushered towards him with Rocky in tow. 'I've got it here. It's about a half hour's drive from here. What's going on?'

'It won't take that long with the blues on. Rocky, get a patrol car round there immediately and explain you'll be following,' Hamilton demanded. 'If what Claire Newcomb's just said is true, then Walker's our killer. I want you and Rocky to follow the patrol car now and secure the house once she's been arrested.'

The two men set off instantly, without another word of questioning. Hamilton wiped his brow as Fraser called out that she had the Cumbrian Inspector waiting on the line.

'Bennett, excuse my directness, but this is a matter of urgency,' he hollered after he'd snatched the receiver from Fraser's hand. 'Did you send officers round to that address in Keswick I gave you?'

'Good afternoon to you too, Detective Inspector.' The man's thick accent droned in Hamilton's ear, each passing second felt like a gruelling minute. 'I thought it an unusual request, but my superior cleared it without a second's thought. You really must have friends in high places, Hamilton. Do you usually only have to snap your fingers and –'

'Bennett!'

'Yes, yes, good God, man, calm down. I have two of my best PCSOs at the address now.'

Hamilton spent a few minutes updating Bennett about the progress they'd made on the Warren Speed case. He also explained, as Holly Walker's adoptive mother resided in the Lake District, they could find a clue there regarding Donna Moran's disappearance. He demanded a full search of Monica Summers' property. Bennett had the good sense to listen without interrupting Hamilton, and when he replied, there appeared to be no sarcasm in the man's tone any longer.

'Right, well, that does alter things. I'll call my officers and ensure they do not leave the house. Then, I'll head over there myself and oversee everything.'

'Exactly what I was hoping you'd say, Inspector. Monica Summers explained to my mother she receives regular letters from one of her adopted daughters, asking if the old woman still lives at that address. Her continued interest in confirming that fact bugs me. There must be something of importance to her in that house.'

'We'll conduct a thorough search of the house, Hamilton, rest assured.'

'Keep me updated on my mobile if anything appears out of place. Please.'

Hamilton added the final word as a courtesy before ending the call. Although he knew he shouldn't feel like he was asking for a favour, it became difficult to dismiss that feeling. However, Bennett would want a conviction, as much as he needed a solution to these intertwined cases, and therefore had to be confident he'd receive their utmost cooperation. However, the huge distance between police forces frustrated him, and the fact he couldn't oversee every aspect of the case caused his temper to rear its ugly head. He kicked out at a near-by rubbish bin just as Dixon entered the office.

'Newcomb give you any more information?' he asked.

'Oh yeah, she's singing like a bloody canary now. Amazing the power an interview room can hold over some people.'

Hamilton called Fraser to join them and bring herself up to speed with recent developments, so as not to continually repeat himself. He then gestured with his hand for Dixon to resume.

'It would appear Warren Speed was a naughty boy, playing away from home with his personal assistant, Claire. She said Holly had snapped some incriminating pictures of the two of them together and has been blackmailing her ever since. Not wanting it to leak to the press, Felicity, or her own boyfriend, Claire organised the trip to Ambleside and orchestrated for Warren to meet Holly at the old boat house after closing time. She stayed away until instructed to return the next morning, but swears blind she no idea the meet-up would lead to murder.'

'Where does the brother, Jason, fit into all of this?' Fraser asked.

Dixon perched on a desk. 'Holly had been dating him for the past six months. He was older than her, by about ten years, and Claire explained he'd never had a steady girlfriend, barely went out on dates, for that matter. Although she could see Holly was using her brother, she didn't know to what extent until very recently.'

'So, Holly manipulated the man in order to get him to steal the vials of botulinum toxin from his place of work. She needed the bigger doses of poison to overpower, kill, and torture Warren Speed and Felicity Ireland,' Hamilton surmised.

'It's how the story seems to be unfolding,' Dixon continued. 'Except Claire found it strange from the get-go because, from discussions with Warren, she assumed Holly was gay. I would venture a bet that due to Jason's lack of confidence, Holly's attention towards him and even just the promise of sex, may have been all she needed to force this man to bend to her will.'

Fraser clicked her fingers. 'Perhaps Holly was in a secret relationship with Donna Moran and blamed the other two for her disappearance, so decided to get revenge.'

Hamilton thought of the remaining friends. 'You could be on to something there. And if that is the case, Holly Walker might just blame all her friends. Fraser, organise a couple of patrol cars to go out to Todd and Calvin. They could be her next victims.'

* * *

Within the next half an hour, Hamilton had received two critical phone calls. Inspector Bennett's grave voice informed him the remains of a young woman had been uncovered in Monica Summers' attic. The team struggled to open the hatch door in the ceiling, but the stench indicated all was not right in the house.

'Do you think Summers had something to do with it?' Hamilton questioned.

'God, no, the old woman's oblivious. The ground floor is neat and tidy and smells of flowers,' Bennett explained. 'If you didn't climb the stairs to the top floor, no one would be any the wiser that the smell of death lingered upstairs.'

'Well, I'd question her anyway. Apart from Jason's assistance, we're assuming Holly Walker worked alone, but who knows how many people she's been manipulating. Let's not take anything for granted.'

'The woman can't lift a foot up the stairs, Hamilton, I saw that with my own two eyes. Anyway, the attic is completely empty, except for the skeleton in the pink dress, of course.'

His Cumbria counterpart continued to assure him a thorough investigation of the house was currently underway. Amy Sullivan, the pathologist Hamilton had spoken to last week, was already combing through the crime scene, and Bennett promised his top priority was to identify the victim. Hamilton's stomach churned, knowing a formal identification was unnecessary at this point.

Donna Moran had been found. His thoughts sped to the young girl's mother. While the forthcoming news would be heart wrenching, he took comfort in the fact his team could finally offer the woman some kind of peace of mind. At least now, a mother could say goodbye to her daughter, and lay her body to rest.

Clarke, on the other hand, informed him they'd lost their person of interest. The sirens alerted Holly Walker to their advance, and she'd run from her home. Last seen near Fulham Broadway, in a crowd of home fans in town for the evening's Chelsea match.

'Advise the uniformed officers in the area about our runner,' Hamilton demanded. 'I appreciate the vicinity will be swamped right now, but I want extra surveillance at all the nearest train stations, in case she tries to slip away. Myself and Dixon will make our way over to you.'

'That's not all, gov,' Clarke added. 'We found Todd Bell gagged and bound to a wooden table in a large shed at the bottom of Walker's very overgrown garden.'

'I bloody knew it. She's on some kind of vendetta. Is he alive?'

'Barely. He's been drugged, but the ambulance is already on the way to the hospital with him.'

Hamilton frowned. 'We haven't heard back from the patrol car we sent out to Calvin Robinson, so scratch what I said before. He lives and works near the station. I'm going to try and hunt him down.'

'There's no way Walker could have got to him in the time she left her house,' Clarke said. 'Unless she already had him tied up somewhere else.'

'It's possible,' he hesitated. 'But perhaps the reason we can't find him is because he's been in on this with Walker the entire time.'

With clear plans, Hamilton ended the call and instructed Fraser to contact ANPR, anxious Holly could have somehow double backed on his team and collected her car.

'Also, see if you can do anything with local CCTV in the area,' he suggested. 'I know, I know, there's a bloody Chelsea match preparing to kick off, and the roads are manic. But we have to try everything we can.'

Fraser's fingers danced along her keyboard, and she called a near-by sergeant for extra help. 'Leave it with me, boss. You'll be the first to hear if I find anything.'

'Right, Dixon, you're with me. As uniform have had no luck at his home address, let's see if we can hunt down the elusive Calvin Robinson at work.'

She followed him through the incident room, easily keeping up with his long strides. 'Doesn't he work near the station?'

'Yes, and he gave us the slip last time. We'll take the car, but be prepared to chase after this one.'

Dixon overtook him and pushed the door wide open. 'I'm always prepared, boss.'

As Hamilton parked the car outside the coffee shop, Dixon tugged on his arm, stopping him from getting out of the car.

'Look, there's our guy leaving,' she said and pointed to the young man who'd just pulled his signature cap further down his head.

Hamilton glanced at Dixon. 'Thinking what I'm thinking?'

'Let's abandon the car here and see where he's off to in such a hurry.'

He clicked his tongue in approval and exited the car. Dixon grabbed her mobile from her pocket and kept her head down most of the way. She discreetly looked up to dodge oncoming tourists and commuters, before returning her attention to her hand. Hamilton liked her style, she looked like every other pedestrian engrossed in their phone. He stayed a few yards behind her, concerned that if Calvin looked back and caught sight of him, they'd be caught. He was surprised when, just seven minutes later, Calvin descended the steps towards Embankment station. Dixon fell back in line with Hamilton.

'Shit, boss, we're going to lose him if he goes in there.'

'Hang back for a minute and don't take your eyes off him. He might not actually be going inside the station.'

'What makes you think that?'

'The district line runs through this station, and can be picked up from Parsons Green in Fulham.'

'Looks like she did give our boys the slip earlier than Clarke thought,' Dixon said and slightly nodded at the entrance as Holly Walker exited.

'Stay this side. I'm going to try and get behind them,' Hamilton said, before slinking off through the crowd.

Yards away from the couple, Hamilton froze when he noticed the glistening object peeking from the sleeve of Holly's jacket. His mind raced, contemplating how he could get the civilians away in the safest manner. But, as Holly's eyes locked with his, he knew it was too late. He jumped forward, knocking innocent members of the public back and hopefully away from the murdering maniac.

'Police! Drop your weapon,' he yelled.

In one swift motion, Holly kicked Calvin behind the knee, causing him to drop to the ground. She lowered the knife into her hand and tugged it against the man's throat, warning everyone to stay away. Screams echoed through the street and the ticket hall of the station. People pushed and struggled against each other to move further away.

In his peripheral vision, Hamilton spied Dixon taking a step back and joining the crowd. Camouflaged by those surrounding her, she discreetly made a phone call, and he knew his team were being notified. He only wondered would the back-up make it in time before another person's life was robbed.

CHAPTER TWENTY-EIGHT

I catch him out of the corner of my eye; he must think I'm stupid. That fucking copper gets everywhere. Calvin could have been my ticket out of here; he has friends aboard. The mere mention of being in a spot of bother, we'd have been on a plane out of here. Men are easy to manipulate. But sadly, my hand's been forced, and Calvin will have to help me another way.

With the knife held firmly against his neck, a trickle of blood falls down his skin, and Calvin begs and pleads with me. He's confused, as always. Never was the brightest spark out of all us, forever trying to please everyone, wanting to be accepted by everyone. He was the only one who helped me look for Donna the year after she disappeared. It would have been his saving grace.

'Holly, what the fuck are you doing?' he shouts, but it sounds like a baby whining.

'Shut it, Cal. I don't want to have to hurt you, but I will.' I say it through gritted teeth, hoping the copper doesn't hear me. 'Don't fight against me and you won't get hurt. Just follow my lead, and you'll never hear from me again.'

Lucky for him, he does as I say. The bloke, Hamilton I think his name is, tiptoes closer to us, his hands held out at his waist, and I shout for him to stand back. Another man who does as he's told. It gives me a chance to scan the area and plan some kind of escape. That's when I see her, the tall, tanned goddess I'd locked eyes with the last time I was at the police station. Such a shame she's on their side. I bet she's amazing in bed.

People are screaming. It's not like I've got a gun pointed at them, calm the fuck down. This is about me now, and how I'm going to get out of here. I still haven't found the answers I'm looking for, and there's no way I'm going down before I have. In the distance, sirens collide with the shrieking noise of those now filming us.

This is not how I'd planned it. This is not how things were supposed to work out.

'Holly, drop your weapon. We can talk about this.'

The mixed-race detective is at it again. Encroaching on my space. Pretending to be my friend so I'll come quietly.

The saliva drains from my mouth, yet my head is full of work-out sweat. I feel grounded, rooted in this indecisive spot for hours, rather than minutes.

It's now or never.

'Keep him down,' I mutter in Calvin's ear, and launch him from his crouching position on top of the copper.

My mate comes through and squashes the fucker to the ground. More screams erupt from the crowd. I've never been watched like this. A tingling sensation erupts in my stomach, shooting lightning bolts of pleasure down between my legs.

She steps forward, the gorgeous brunette, and I see the look in her eye. The hunger. She won't let me pass without a fight, but the movement behind tells me the other copper will be on my heels in minutes. Slipping the knife into my left hand, I wait for her to gain momentum, charging at me like a thunderous deity. Throwing a right hook, hard and fast, she falls back and smacks her head on the cold, concrete steps.

The pathetic onlookers, adding their own drama with squeals and gasps, step away. But, you know there's always one have-a-go-hero, who thinks he can take someone like me on. Not today, fuckers. I lift the knife, wield it around, and slice it through the air like a crazy samurai warrior. They run away, scared for their lives. As if I have time for them.

I climb the stairs to freedom and listen to him calling the name Dixon repeatedly. He won't stick around; no one is that loyal to the people they work with. The thrill of the chase will entice him. I think I'd like to play a game with him, but not today.

They must have found Todd in my shed. That bitch Claire will have spilled her guts, and so, they have all they need on me. I'm used to hiding, it's what I do best. I'm well equipped to conceal myself in plain sight to save my own skin. Once the dust settles, I'll come back for Donna.

I carefully slip the knife back up the arm of my jacket and leg it, doubling back on myself, away from Victoria Embankment. Even here, away from the picturesque river I have to swerve through crowds of tossers stopping to take selfies. As I run along Northumberland Avenue and Trafalgar Square, panting and out of breath, the doors of a red, double decker bus close in my face. I bang, just the once, and the Asian driver reopens them. I jump on, without thinking of where I could end up.

'That was very kind of you. Most drivers leave me standing there like an idiot.'

I reach for the contactless bank card in my back pocket and let it beep on the terminal. The doors slam shut as the driver pulls away. I take the first seat, next to old woman who smiles sweetly at me. I return the gesture. After all, wouldn't you be laughing if you'd just escaped for the second time in one evening.

'This is the 453, to Deptford Bridge Station.' The automated female voice announces over the speaker.

Fuck knows what I'll do in Deptford, if I even go that far, but I've got some breathing space. Some time to plan my next move.

CHAPTER TWENTY-NINE

Hamilton raced back to the train station, the scene looking completely different in the short time he'd been gone. Dixon, who forced him to chase Holly the second she opened her eyes, now sat in the back of an ambulance, being treated by two young paramedics. Clarke and Rocky, who were returning to the station, were given the update by Fraser and diverted to Victoria Embankment. Calvin Robinson sat in the back of a stationary patrol car, his face contorted and nostrils flaring.

Commuters moaned and demanded answers about when the station would reopen. Hamilton could understand their frustrations and realised their restraints only caused more problems. The area was no longer a crime scene, their suspect had given them the slip, and SOCO were rendered unnecessary. He rushed forward, recognising time was against them.

'We're wasting our resources here. Pull down the barriers and let these people continue with their evening,' he urged, and turned to face his team. 'I couldn't catch Walker, but I sure as hell caught up with her. She didn't notice me following her.'

Hamilton explained the escape route Holly had taken, and wondered if she'd have the audacity to only journey one or two stops before jumping off the bus.

'We need to get ahead of her.'

'Let me have a quick think.' Clarke paused. 'From here, the 453 will run along the Horse Guards Palace … onto Westminster and Parliament Square, before heading past St Thomas's Hospital …'

'Right, let's head over to the hospital. We can get there in about six minutes,' Hamilton shouted, and ran towards Clarke's car, delighted someone knew the inner workings of the London bus routes. To him, the large, red vehicles all merged into one as they criss-crossed over lanes and swam around roundabouts in their droves. 'I want all patrols in the vicinity with us, but keep your sirens off. If she twigs any sign of us, we risk losing her, *again.*'

Clarke started the engine and sped off along the River Thames. He switched the lights on, but kept them silenced. They just had to get over the bridge, Hamilton thought, hoping their close proximity to the hospital would beat the bus's longer route around the city.

'What if Walker's already off the bus?' Clarke asked, as he expertly whizzed through the evening traffic.

'Then we're up shit creek, partner. She could be anywhere in this city right now.'

Big Ben filled their view as Clarke sped along Westminster Pier, before taking a left onto Westminster Bridge Road. As always, the footpath and roads brimmed with pedestrians and traffic. The silent siren had its advantages, however, and slowly cars pulled aside to let them pass, without drawing too much attention to their chase. An array of police cars joined the bridge from different directions. As they advanced on St Thomas's Hospital, Hamilton saw some were already in place, dotted around the side streets of Belvedere and York Road. Confident they had beaten the 453 to this destination, he instructed Clarke to switch off the lights and park directly at the bus stop.

Hamilton opened the door before Clarke came to a screeching halt, and jogged back on himself, wanting a better view of the bridge. In the distance, like a beacon of everything British, a red double decker drew closer towards them. Although he couldn't make out the numbers on the front, hope won over. It was all he had.

'Get everyone in position,' he instructed Clarke, who joined him near the bridge. 'Tell Rocky to stay in the patrol car, and cover the rear of the bus after it stops. Tell everyone to keep back, but be prepared.'

Clarke darted back to the teams, as Hamilton's impatience grew. He thought about approaching the bus as it crawled along the bridge in the traffic, but he didn't want to put anyone on the vehicle in harm's way. If they played it discreetly, he had a chance of getting on the bus before Holly realised he was there. His focus narrowed in and read the numbers 453 in bold, white lettering, and he thumped his fist in jubilation while running back to the bus stop.

It pulled to a halt, and the mechanical doors swung open. The driver's face grew aghast as Hamilton jumped on-board, flashed his ID card, and placed his index finger over his lips. Clarke and two uniformed officers approached the middle doors, scanned the passengers alighting, while Hamilton climbed the stairs two at a time. Examining every bewildered and puzzled face, he soon realised Holly was not on the top deck.

'Gov, down here,' his partner called up to him.

Hamilton almost tripped down the narrow stairs as he bombed his way back down. He sighed a breath of relief when he found Clarke standing on the street alone, the officers must have placed their suspect in a near-by patrol car.

'Wrong flaming bus,' Clarke said and pointed to the second red double decker a few yards behind; Hamilton hadn't even noticed it on the bridge. 'Walker saw all the commotion and legged it down Belvedere Road, a no-through-way for cars. Rocky and a couple of officers are in pursuit now.'

Hamilton swung round and punched the bus behind him, livid the woman had evaded their clutches one more.

* * *

Rocky lost sight of the two uniformed policemen who'd followed Holly Walker with him. It wasn't that he'd describe them as overweight, but thinking back to his last chase with Hamilton, he wondered if it would be beneficial to reopen the old gym at the station. He'd passed by the shell of a basement last week, disappointed the machines and weights had been abandoned to collect dust. He appreciated that many people now paid hefty monthly gym memberships, which could become a nightmare to get out of. But why neglect a perk of the job situated in the very building you worked in every day, he thought. Running along the tall, white buildings of Belvedere Road, he decided he'd proposition Hamilton about his idea.

As the road in front began to open up, a line of black taxis came into view. Worried Holly would jump in the nearest vehicle and become lost in a convoy of beetles, Rocky ran from the pavement and into the middle of the road to keep an eye on her. His speed increased, muscular legs taking the strain as he bolted past, yelling at innocent bystanders to move out of his way.

Holly constantly peered over her shoulder as she slowed down, fingers reaching out to grab the handle of the nearest black taxi. The door remained locked, and Rocky watched her yank harder and harder, knocking the window while checking the progress he made on her.

'Police! Holly Walker, stop!' he yelled, and pedestrians instantly backed away from him.

She leaned into the taxi window, demanding the driver open the door, and the woman's hesitation became Rocky's victory. His strides transformed into huge leaps from the ground. He extended his arm and grasped her shoulder, tackling her to the ground.

'Holly Walker, you are under arrest,' Rocky said and continued with the apprehension as he handcuffed her wrists behind her back.

Adjusting his position to notify the team, Rocky inhaled sharply when he noticed the iconic grandness of The London Eye. Since moving to the city, he'd promised himself to visit the popular sites – not just from a distance. He wanted to get up, close and personal with each and every one. Take a dozen photos of the same scene, just so he didn't miss anything about the wonderful sites. Now, he gazed in awe, feeling like a dwarf under the giant, white metal wheel towering over the buildings and trees. It's numerous pods, each holding dozens of people, soared so high he thought they might just pass through the few clouds surrounding them. He strained his neck to follow the circular attraction as Holly wriggled beneath him.

'Get off me. I'll sue,' she screamed, venom spitting from her lips. 'Look at all these people recording you. You'll be done for this, mark my words, you piece of filth.'

Rocky sighed, the beauty of the city tarnished by the criminals inhabiting it. He ignored the woman's continued outbursts and reached for his phone. The two uniformed officers joined him, and promptly guided back the crowd of people who had come to watch with interest, their mobiles held high to capture every second of the excitement unfolding before them.

'Put those phones away, and step back now!' the older of the two policemen demanded.

Rocky followed the direction of the man's voice and spotted Hamilton tearing down the street towards him. He slipped his phone back into his pocket, placed his hands under Holly's armpits and scooped her up from the ground.

'Careful where you're putting those bloody things,' she roared.

He ignored her comment once again and gestured his head towards his boss. Hamilton's feet slowed slightly, but the pearls of brimming sweat and deep frown lines on his forehead told Rocky the intensity remained.

'Well done. Bloody well done,' Hamilton said and slapped him on the back. 'You're getting some reputation for a successful chase, I'll give you that.'

'Thanks, boss. I work out.'

Hamilton laughed heartily. 'No need to rub it in, mate, we can all see that.'

'What's this all about?' Holly interrupted, but she no longer screamed, rather her tone sounded steady, and the vein in her temple pulsated. 'You've got nothing on me.'

'We have witnesses,' Hamilton replied.

'Ha! Fucking witnesses. You lot would believe the first person who walked in off the street if they told you what you wanted to hear.'

'Let's see about that down the station, shall we. Rocky, the patrol cars can't drive up here so, rather than waiting for them to drive around, let's get her back down Belvedere Road.'

Together, they took an arm each and guided Holly in the direction they wanted, not that she struggled or fought against them. Rocky felt as if he was walking on air, strutting down the street while Hamilton's words played repeatedly in his mind. He couldn't remember the last time someone in a senior position called him "mate," and it tickled him. More and more, he believed the move to London had been a positive change in his life, and the team he worked with were not just colleagues, they were friends.

CHAPTER THIRTY

Hamilton shuddered. A chill snaked down his back, and the small hairs on his neck stood to attention. Unsure if the coldness came from the damp room or the monster sat in front of him, he pulled his suit jacket closer together and fastened the buttons. Dixon accompanied him in the interview, purely because he'd liked the technique and unsympathetic nature she'd adopted while questioning Todd Bell. He wanted answers from Holly Walker, and wasn't prepared to pussyfoot around the suspect. In their absence, Fraser had been tasked with discovering everything she could from Inspector Bennett about the girl in the Ambleside attic. If information could be sourced during this initial interview with Holly, Hamilton believed a full confession would come easy.

He watched her for a few moments; the way her eyes, dark as the midnight sky, scrutinised the room and her pale cheek twitched, as if she was biting the inside of her mouth. Now Holly had shed her jacket, Hamilton could see the bulging muscles in the woman's large arms. Within the space of three minutes, she'd run a hand through her cropped, red hair, flicking it over and covering one side of her forehead, at least ten times. Yet, despite her tense actions, he could feel a calmness radiating from her body. She relaxed back into the plastic chair, leaning on the arm rests, and her feet placed firmly on the floor, legs uncrossed. Without a care in the world, Holly showed no remorseful or anxious emotion, Hamilton thought.

After Dixon had stated all the necessary information for the recording, Hamilton revealed all his cards, explaining all the details they'd gathered on Holly. The woman chuckled at the mention of Claire Newcomb's name, and confessed how much she regretted not silencing the snitch when she had the chance.

'It's a real shame about Jason though,' Holly continued. 'He wasn't a bad guy, just wanted someone to love him. Don't we all, hey?' She laughed again and chucked a wink in Dixon's direction.

'But you didn't love him, did you? Rather, you manipulated a self-conscious man and forced him to commit suicide,' Hamilton retorted.

'Ah, yes, I Googled you while on that damned bus, detective. Read all about your daughter and how she was forced to do something she didn't want to do. Or did she? See, I believe we make our own chances in this world, and some people are just weaker than others.'

Hamilton stared into the heartless woman's black eyes and drew on something from deep inside. A serenity he had recently granted himself, knowing he couldn't have stopped Maggie's decision to take her own life. But he could rid this city of evil, one criminal at a time.

'And you enjoy using weak people, don't you, Holly? There's no way you would have been able to steal all the vials of Botox you needed to poison both Warren Speed and Felicity Ireland. Is that correct?'

She shrugged and rolled her head, the bones clicking in her neck audible to everyone. 'I did what I had to do, Detective. Sometimes, not only the weak are forced to do things. I know how it feels to be used, and it can bring heart-aching pain. But karma is a bitch, as they say.'

He rubbed his forefinger and thumb along his goatee and glared at the round, plump face of pure evil. The ugliness of the woman's soul most certainly mirrored the unpleasantness of her external features.

'We also know about Donna Moran,' he said, deciding to prod the beast.

Holly's mouth opened and closed before she stuttered, 'Really? What have you found?'

'Give it up. We've found her body. You can drop the act.'

'I just … I can't believe you've finally found her. I've been …' she trailed off.

Hamilton's eyes squinted together. 'Did you really think we'd never find her? Your adoptive mother's house was about to be sold. It was only a matter of time.'

Holly raised her head, a smirk danced across her face. 'I hate to burst your bubble, Detective, but I'm afraid you haven't found Donna.'

She ran a hand through her short hair and looked away. Hamilton watched the change happen right in front of his eyes; as though she'd previously been possessed with the ghost of sadness, only now to be replaced by a demon of evil. Holly placed her elbows on the table, cupped her hands together and rested her chin on top, looking like the master in a business meeting. Her eyes no longer brimmed with expectant tears, but were mere slits, her focus returned to Hamilton. He wouldn't allow her brazen façade to confuse him, and he mirrored her actions, sitting forward and looking directly at her.

'I see you prefer to play games, Miss Walker. There's really no need. We have a team of specialists at your previous address and we know about the body in the attic.'

'I'm not disputing there's a body in the attic, Detective. I put it there. I'm just telling you it's not Donna.'

'It sounds like you don't really want to stop there. You seem to have all the information. Why don't you enlighten us?'

She sat back in the chair and sighed. 'The woman you found is Becky Taylor, my adoptive sister. She's been in the attic for …' Holly groaned, '… five years now.'

He tightened his jaw, adamant not to highlight his shock at the woman's directness. 'And you murdered Becky Taylor, why?'

Holly rolled her eyes to the ceiling, ignoring his question, when Dixon sat forward. 'You were in a relationship with your adoptive sister, weren't you?'

Hamilton suddenly remembered the information Claire had shared about the suspect's sexual orientation and watched Holly with curiosity. She eyed Dixon and licked her lips.

'I bet you'd love to hear all about that, wouldn't you, Sergeant.' Holly's cackle filled the room.

'Answer the damn question,' Dixon replied.

Holly tutted. 'Pretty face but that demanding mouth will get you nowhere quick.'

'Well, let me apologise for my mouth. You're right. I'd love to hear all about you and Becky. Why don't you tell me?'

Holly's menacing smirk returned to play, and Hamilton could think of nothing better than wiping it off the murderer's face. He hated the long, drawn-out route they were taking with the woman, half wanting to leave the interview room and discover for himself if she were telling the truth. But he could see a twinkle in Holly's eye when she looked at Dixon, so he decided to sit back and stay quiet for once.

'I was fifteen when I first stepped foot into the Summers' house,' Holly explained, gazing intently at Dixon. 'They were a nice enough couple, though I hated the idea of living out in the sticks. But then, they introduced me to Becky, and said we could share a bedroom, if I wanted, to help me settle in. She was eighteen … beautiful and kind, and actually interested in *me*. I didn't know what I was feeling that first moment I saw her … I'd never felt it before. It was tingly and exciting, and I felt alive for the first time in my shitty, disgusting life.

'Over the years, we grew closer than sisters. I'd do anything for her, and she for me. I soon realised it was love I had felt the moment I laid eyes on Becky Taylor. A blonde bombshell. An angel to protect me. And gosh, she taught me some things,' Holly paused to laugh. Rubbing a hand up and down her arm, she stared intently at the table before continuing.

'In an instant, it all changed. Becky didn't want to spend time with me anymore, said I was too young and immature. It was all a lie, you see, because I followed her one evening and found her shagging some bastard in the backseat of his car. Suddenly, it was all, "I'm moving to Scotland." and "I'm going to start a family with Patrick." It was a fucking joke. She used me, until she found the next thing she was interested in playing with …'

Dixon cleared her throat, gaining Holly's attention once again. 'But why kill her and leave her in Monica Summers' attic?'

'Because she thought she could abandon me there,' Holly spat. 'I gave her a chance, more than one, to change her mind. To tell me she'd made a mistake, and she loved me and would stay with me. She showed her true colours, and I knew then it wasn't love at all, just infatuation. The bitch deserved to die.'

'Is that what happened with Donna Moran too?' Hamilton joined in. 'Did she betray you and abandon you too?'

She sucked in a lungful of air. 'Ah, now that is love. Donna was never ready, but she was honest. We toyed with each other. I aroused more than just her interests, but I promised I'd wait. Some people need to get it out of their system, be with a few men to know it's not really for them. That's what Donna was doing but with my consent.'

'So, where did it all go wrong?'

'Warren Speed and his overactive cock, is where it all went wrong, Detective.'

'And that made you mad?'

Holly swayed her head from side to side and turned down her lips. 'He wasn't the only one. Donna was playing away with an older, married man at Brunel, but I allowed her to indulge herself. After all, those are the years we're expected to find ourselves. But with Warren … I began to worry she was falling for him. That night in Ambleside, when she agreed to stay at the boat house, the anger inside of me … Well, let's just say, I've never been so consumed. She was being stupid, showing off in front of that bell end. I told you the truth before. I wasn't interested in the dare and left. But guilt took over. How could I leave the woman I love out there alone? That's when I saw the two of them together, Warren and Felicity, fucking each other in the middle of the forest like their lives depended on it. I thought, if Donna saw them together, she'd understand what I'd been trying to tell her about him. But the boat house was already empty when I got there.'

'And you blamed Warren and Felicity for Donna running away?'

'She did not run away,' Holly yelled. 'Donna would not have left me without a word. We lied; she didn't leave a note explaining anything. Yes, her bags had gone the next morning, but she hadn't explained why. Warren forced us to tell that story to the police two years ago, because he said we'd look guilty otherwise. I've spent all this time looking for Donna, investigating the happy couple and following their every move. When they announced their engagement six months ago, I finally snapped. Together, they got rid of Donna so they could be with each other.'

Hamilton frowned. 'Did you find any evidence that Warren and Felicity killed your friend? Because this really could be a runaway case. Perhaps she had also seen the pair together in the forest before you went to find her; it was too much to handle, and she decided to leave.'

'No! Not at all. I will never believe that. I knew Donna better than she knew herself. Don't you two have any friends, or lovers?' Holly said and looked between Hamilton and Dixon. 'There are people in this world we understand, without the need for words and explanations. And Donna is that person to me. She would not have ignored me, and her own mother, for all this time. I know she's dead.'

'And you admit to murdering Warren Speed and Felicity Ireland in order to try and find out what happened to Donna Moran,' Dixon stated.

Holly crossed her arms over her large breasts. 'Yes, I did. They wouldn't tell me where they hid her body, but they deserved to feel pain. To cry and beg. To litter the dirty rivers, just the way they left Donna to. The pair deserved to fucking die.'

Dixon officially arrested Holly for the murders, while Hamilton's left leg jerked underneath the table, forward thinking about the next warrant his team would need, and the courage he'd need to search for.

'Interview terminated,' he declared, and sprinted from the room.

CHAPTER THIRTY-ONE

The team, accompanied by uniformed officers and forensic scientists, marched into William Thorn's home little over an hour after Hamilton left the interview room. While his old friend and Dorinda were detained in the kitchen with the FLO, everyone else bustled through every room, pulling out drawers and cupboards, searching the attic and basement and collecting DNA. He wasn't sure what they'd find, but Hamilton was adamant this family house homed the secret to Donna Moran's disappearance.

'What are you doing?' Dorinda moaned. 'The girl just ran away. Why in God's name would you find anything here?

Hamilton glanced in Billy's direction and spied the look of pure desperation in his eyes. With the slightest movement of his head, Billy shook it from side to side and clenched his jaw.

'That's why you really came to see me, wasn't it?' Hamilton said, ignoring Dorinda's question. 'You wanted to know if I had anything on you after we'd re-opened Donna's investigation. That's why you were creeping around, slinking in the shadows around my home.'

'No.'

'What do you mean?' Dorinda questioned again, vying for attention.

His attention remained on Billy. 'You thought you could play the old friendship card and pull the wool over my eyes, didn't you, *mate*?'

'You've got it all wrong,' Billy whispered.

'Really? But, you were having an affair with Donna Moran, weren't you? You're the older man at Brunel she had a fling with.

Why you acted shifty when I asked how well you knew her, and the real reason she visited your office.'

Billy closed his eyes and fell back onto a dining chair. Dorinda gasped and looked down at her pale partner, shaking her head.

'We've contacted the university and have asked them to collect CCTV footage from the day Donna went missing, after she'd left Ambleside,' Hamilton lied, but he knew his only chance of a confession was to back his old friend into a corner.

'From two years ago, surely they wouldn't still –'

'Oh, there's every possibility they'll still have the footage, Dorinda, especially on a campus as vast as Brunel.' He refocused on Billy. 'You told me you didn't see Donna after she'd returned from the Lakes, but you were lying.'

Billy finally looked at Hamilton, but remained silent.

'Dorinda hadn't long since given birth to your daughter. Perhaps you wanted to end the affair, and Donna didn't like the idea. Didn't want to let you go.'

'No, it's not –'

'So, your original story is unwavering? You see, I think you did see her before she vanished. And I have my suspicions that she isn't a runaway case at all. Donna Moran, recently graduated, extremely popular and social media mad, suddenly goes off the grid for two years. For what reason? It just doesn't make sense to me.' Hamilton paused, walked around the table and folded his arms. 'Now, I didn't realise this, but since 2014, the use of contactless card payments and terminals has grown in its millions. Did you know that, Billy? My bank card doesn't have that function, although it expires this year, so I'm sure I'll be dragged up to date then.'

'What does this have to do with anything?' Dorinda frowned.

'I'm glad you asked.' Hamilton struck a finger in the air. 'You see, my team are great at hunting things down, and they know their stuff. It took some doing, given we're trying to trace records from two years ago, but Donna Moran's bank finally had something for my Sergeant. After she left Ambleside, her contactless card was used on the London Underground. She touched out at Uxbridge Train Station, and that's the last time the card was ever used. Billy, are you certain she didn't visit you on campus that evening?'

Billy muttered inaudibly, but the following silence spoke volumes to Hamilton.

'You made her go away for good, didn't you?'

'No.'

'Donna threatened to expose your sordid affair.'

'No.'

'Tell your family. Ruin your life.'

'No, it wasn't like that!' Billy's voice rose, and he rubbed his temples.

Hamilton stepped forward, the words spilling from his mouth as fast as his heart beat inside his chest. 'You were about to lose everything you'd worked so hard for, your family, your job, your reputation as a counsellor.'

'No!'

'What did you do, Billy? Strangle her?'

'I would never.'

'But you would shag her, wouldn't you?'

'That was two years ago,' Dorinda screamed, and jumped in front of Billy. 'That bitch tried to rip our family apart, but I wouldn't let her win.' As the final word escaped her lips, Dorinda fell to her knees, panting and crying, and she gripped onto Billy's leg. 'I did it for you. I did it for us, and Amelia. Our family. But I promise it was an accident. It was never meant to go that far. You understand, don't you?'

Billy jumped from his seat and yanked Dorinda's hands from him. Eyes wide, he paced around the small kitchen table and shook his head, like a nodding-dog toy sat on the backseat of a car. He looked from Dorinda to Hamilton and back to his partner.

'No. I can't believe this … what have you done?'

The woman sniffed, wiping her sleeve over the mesh of tears. 'I saw Donna, that night, leaving your office. You were meant to be meeting me in an hour, and I came early to surprise you. I knew you'd slept with the slut while I was pregnant, but I forgave you. I could understand; I never wanted sex. Christ sake, I didn't even want to be touched. I hated being pregnant. You were just satisfying your needs, and it wouldn't last.'

Billy knelt on the floor next to Dorinda and cupped her face in his hands. 'You knew?'

'Of course I did!' she shrieked. 'All those late nights you were working, what a ridiculous lie. It's the oldest one in the book. I followed you some nights. I saw everything. After Amelia was born, I had such an awful time.'

'I remember.'

'Whatever I tried, there was just no connection between my daughter and me. She cried all the time, demanded my attention. But you, you were so loving and generous and helpful. I just knew you'd finished playing away, I knew you loved me. So, that night, when I saw her …'

Astonished, Hamilton stepped forward. 'Why did Donna visit your office that night, Billy?'

His old friend shook his head briefly, as if to recall the memory through the murky revelation he'd just witnessed. 'She was distraught after seeing Warren and Felicity together. She'd headed back to London on the first train she could and was a complete mess.' He paused, removed his hold on Dorinda and stood up. 'It was over between us already. It was over the moment my daughter was born. I'm sorry, but you didn't see what you think you saw that night. Donna purely needed a shoulder to cry on.'

As Billy backed away from his partner, Hamilton took his place and towered over the crying wreck of a woman.

'I never wanted Felicity to be friends with that girl,' she sobbed. 'I warned her Donna was bad news. I could see it in her evil eyes.'

Hamilton sat on the chair nearest to Dorinda. 'Tell me what happened after Donna left Billy's office.'

She took a deep breath, her eyes fixed on the man she loved. 'I followed her around the back of campus, near the car park, where they were doing some building work. It was late, too dark for anyone to be working at that time of night. I just wanted to have a chat, woman to woman, and tell her to back off. But she was hysterical. Yelling that I didn't deserve a good man like Billy, and how much of a useless mother I was, that I'd be better off in a home, like my own mum.'

Dorinda's wails echoed through the kitchen like a haunting banshee, mumbling as she covered her face with both hands. Her shoulders shook violently, and Billy reached out, his own hand rested on her thigh.

'What happened to Donna after that?'

'I lost it,' she confessed, wiping her face once again. 'I punched her in the face. Just once, I promise. But the force of it knocked her back so hard her head slammed against the kerb. Jesus Christ, if you'd seen the amount of blood … it poured along the road and right down the drain beside her.'

Billy frowned. 'Wait, you called me that night, and we had an argument about you not wanting to go out after all.'

'I panicked. No one would believe it was an accident, once the rumours of your affair bloody got out. For the first time since giving birth, in that moment, I just wanted to hold my baby girl and protect her. I knew if anyone found out, I'd probably never see Amelia, or you, ever again.'

'Amelia was staying with your best friend, and you told me not to come home that night. What did you do with Donna's body?'

While listening to the confession, Hamilton stood up and walked over to the window. Admiring the beauty of their garden, he noticed the patch of grass at the far end where no flowers grew. He called out for Laura Joseph and asked her to examine the back of the house.

'Maintaining and decorating gardens is what you do for a profession, isn't it, Dorinda?' The woman looked to the floor and nodded. 'The break in flower patterns isn't intentional out there, is it? It's where you buried Donna Moran's body.'

The sobs returned while Billy jumped to his feet and raced to the back door. The forensic team had already begun setting up perimeters in preparation of digging the earth.

'No! This can't be true, Dorinda. Our child is asleep upstairs in her cot. Tell me that girl's body has not been buried in our back garden for the last two years.'

'I'm sorry,' she snivelled. 'I didn't know where else to put her … where she wouldn't be found. I never meant for any of this to happen. But I couldn't lose my family.'

'You should have said it was an accident. I would have stood by you. But now, you've lost us all,' Billy spat, and left the room as Amelia's waking cries resonated through the house.

Hamilton requested Dixon and Rocky accompany Dorinda to the station, but asked them to leave her in the cell for the time being; he wanted to be the one to file the official charges against her. Waiting in the kitchen with Clarke, to ensure Donna Moran actually was found in the burial place confessed to, guilt jabbed him in the stomach. The mistake he'd made, accusing Billy of murder, could be unforgiveable, but there was no time to dwell. After all, he'd only been following the clues, he attempted to comfort himself.

It wasn't long before the actions of Laura and the other forensics conveyed a clear message: they'd unearthed the missing girl.

CHAPTER THIRTY-TWO

'I can't believe the missus confessed,' Rocky exclaimed. 'After discovering Holly hadn't killed Donna, I thought for sure it was one of the other friends.'

Hamilton gathered the team together in the incident room for a debrief, after an official interview with Dorinda Ireland. Before they all wrote up their reports for the investigation, he needed to ensure they had all the loose ends tied up. He asked Fraser, who had remained at the station while they made the arrest, to update the team about the girl in the attic at Monica Summers' home.

'Inspector Bennett confirmed the victim's identity from her dental records, and it is Becky Taylor, Holly Walker's adoptive sister,' she explained. 'At this time, the pathologist can't shed much light on the cause of death, as she's still examining the remains, but she's confident the time frame fits with what Holly's already confessed.'

'Any update on Todd Bell's condition?'

Clarke raised his hand. 'He's in intensive care at the moment, going through a course of antitoxin to fight the botulism. The doctor I spoke to briefly believed the treatment had been administered quickly enough to be effective.'

'That's good to know. Well done for getting to the house in time.'

'If only the missing persons case had been investigated in more depth all those years ago, perhaps we wouldn't have had this mess to deal with. More innocent people wouldn't have lost their lives.'

'Clarke, over two hundred thousand Britons disappear every year. So, despite the thirteen million CCTV cameras, the databases and Facebook, local neighbourhood watches and GPS, the MisPer department have a hell of a lot to contend with. For them, Donna Moran was a twenty-one-year-old woman, who left a note saying goodbye.'

'A fake note, forged by Warren Speed, and probably not through guilt but self-preservation and fear.'

'Yes, we know that now, but that couldn't have been clear to the officers at the time. There was no threat to life, no suspicious circumstances … she was simply a young woman who wanted to leave London and start a new life. MisPer can't check the oyster card, or contactless bank statements of every reported missing person to identify their last known location. It would be a minefield.'

'In that case, I suppose it's a small blessing Holly Walker wanted us to know the murders linked to Donna Moran.' Clarke sighed heavily. 'What about your mate, William?'

'There's no evidence Billy was involved in Dorinda's crime; it appears she worked alone. However, who knows what the prosecution might try down the line. What with him having an affair with the girl … they could try and place some blame in his court, pitch the couple as co-conspirators, even.'

'As for Holly, she's been charged with three counts of murder. The story about Becky Taylor's death is still unclear, but it appears Holly snapped when betrayal and abandonment threatened her again. She's confessed, so it will all come out.'

'Holly's suffered a lifetime of those feelings,' Fraser added. 'Before her mother took an overdose, the young girl watched a downward spiral of drugs and prostitution in her own home. Who knows what she may have been forced into. As a grown woman, the rejection and neglect changed her, forced her to believe murder is acceptable.'

Dixon placed both hands on her hips. 'But I don't think Dorinda was an evil woman. She'd suffered a traumatic ordeal. I suffered post-natal depression too, after my second child was born, and it's horrific. My father always taught me that pride comes before a fall, so I reached out to my family and asked for help before it consumed me. I'm not excusing the woman's actions, of course, but I can understand her pain.'

'Clearly it was Dorinda's rage which caused the accident,' Rocky said. 'But the secrets and lies following on from that is what created the monster. I mean, hiding the poor girl's body for two years, knowing what her family and friends were going through. If only Dorinda had trusted the police all those years ago, and explained exactly what happened.'

'She would have been charged with manslaughter,' Dixon replied. 'At the end of the day, she killed an innocent young woman, and she deserves, more than ever now, to be held accountable for her actions.'

Hamilton stepped forward. 'Well, justice has certainly been served, and Donna Moran can be laid to rest at long last.'

'What will happen to Claire Newcomb?' Rocky asked.

'She'll be punished for the part she played in all this, albeit a lesser reprimand for supplying us with the information which resulted in apprehending the real murderer. If we'd known about Holly Walker sooner, more lives could have potentially been saved.'

Dixon sighed. 'Isn't it awful how this all started with Dorinda Ireland, a woman clearly suffering after the birth of her daughter. Perhaps, if she'd received some professional help, none of this would have happened.'

'But it was Holly who murdered three people, and ultimately led Jason to his death,' Rocky said.

'Apart from Becky Taylor, Holly made those choices because of what she *thought* her friends had done to the woman she loved. When, in actual fact, they were as clueless as she was. Dorinda's sister died because she covered up murdering Donna Moran. I guess we never really know who we can trust.'

'Is that what you believe?' Rocky asked. 'I have friends and family who I hold dear to me, who have been with me through everything, and dragged me up when I needed help. I'd bet my life on them. Are you seriously saying you don't have friends who mean the world to you? Friends you'd do anything for.'

Dixon raised an eyebrow. 'No one comes above my children. And while, yes, I understand we all need relationships and friendships in this world, I've learnt even those closest to you can betray you, eventually.' She stopped and laughed. 'I'm not a total bitch, by the way. I have a close circle of friends who I'd do anything for … except kill, unlike Holly Walker. But I'm just saying it's important not to lose ourselves for the sake of others. Some friendships are toxic.'

Hamilton nodded, acknowledging Dixon's sentiments, but his shoulders slumped with the heaviness of remorse and regret. 'Let's call it a night, guys. We can finalise the reports and admin side of things after the weekend. We've deserved the break. And I think we all deserve a pint too. I'm buying the first round.'

'You don't have to tell me twice,' Dixon said and swung her handbag over her shoulder.

Clarke, in hot pursuit of her to the door, called out, 'That's what I like to hear.'

Fraser stood, but declined the offer. 'I'm shattered, boss, but thanks. I need a hot bath and early to bed. See you all on Monday.'

After she'd left the room, Rocky tapped Hamilton's shoulder and motioned to the back of the room with his head. He called out to the other two waiting in the doorway, asking them to carry on to The Duke and Duchess across the road, and that he'd catch up with them. Alone, Rocky retold the incident which happened in Fraser's house, and the dead flowers sent by her estranged friend, Johnny.

'I know I should have explained it more to you when I gave you the CCTV image.'

'Damn, I haven't had a chance to chase that up yet.'

'It's just, with all this talk of friendships and asking for help, I thought it was the right thing to do … telling you,' Rocky said and stared at the floor. 'I hope Fraser doesn't end up hating me.'

Hamilton lightly punched the lad on his arm. 'No, of course she won't. I'll be subtle with her too, because I have noticed a distance from her these past few days. I'll use that to gauge things with her and look at that image in more detail first thing on Monday morning. You've done the right thing, okay?'

'Yeah, sure. Thanks, boss. I feel like a weight has been lifted.'

Rocky walked towards the door, and Hamilton hesitated for a moment, before calling him back. 'Here, take this twenty quid and get the team a drink for me. Tell them I'll be half an hour, or so. There's just something personal I need to deal with first.'

EPILOGUE

Hamilton walked along the path, one he hadn't stepped foot on in years, and tapped the gold knocker on the shiny blue door. The row of detached houses, all identical except for a few individual quirks, such as hanging flower pots or brightly painted doors, mirrored the homes three streets down, where he'd grown up. But this place had been his second home throughout his teenage years, and for quite a while after that.

The door creaked open, and a familiar face greeted him. 'Well, this is a surprise,' her friendly voice sung to him. 'Well, don't stand on bloody ceremony. Come in, come in.'

He closed the door behind him, but she hadn't moved far down the hallway, and their arms rubbed against each other. The place hadn't changed; the same flowery carpet un-matching the paisley wallpaper. It looked just as hideous when he was growing up, but you got away with more decorating faux pas in the eighties.

'Mrs Thorn, it's lovely to see you,' he said, attempting to sound bright and breezy, but knowing the words fell as heavy as cement.

She pinched his cheek, and he was transported back to his late teens. Back to when he and Billy would return from a football match later than promised. Mrs Thorn would light-heartedly reprimand the pair and then offer them a toastie. Discipline never had been her strong suit.

'Would you just look at yourself, Denis Hamilton. You've changed … but you're still the same,' she giggled. 'How stupid does that sound, but do you know what I mean? It must be this new hair you're growing on your chin. What do you kids call them, a goatee? I think it ages you.' She continued to laugh as she crossed her arms over her large chest.

'I was wondering if Billy was staying here with you, Mrs T? You know, now that his home has become …'

'A crime scene? Yes, I know all about it. I still can't quite believe what Dorinda's done. What she put that poor girl's family through … and now her own family? I've told Billy he and Amelia can stay with me forever. It's so lovely to have some life and laughter back in this quiet house. Mind you, I must admit none of that is coming from Billy at the moment. But I was overjoyed when he told me things with you were on the mend. So sad when you had that fall out. Dear friends are important.'

Hamilton frowned. The memory she'd mentioned unbeknown to him, but he couldn't help smiling. Mrs Thorn jabbered on, as he remembered her always doing, and he took a minute to study her face. She'd grown so old, it scared him somewhat. The deep lines around her mouth and eyes had intensified in her grey, sagging skin. The headful of white hair, a stark contrast to the glistening ash brown he recollected. Mrs Thorn was similar in age to his own mother, yet this woman looked at least ten years older. He contemplated if it were due to the fact Mrs Thorn had stayed in London, with all its pressures and anxieties, while Philippa Hamilton relaxed and enjoyed Ambleside, the exhilarating views of Lake Windermere, and the constant flow of fresh air. Obviously, these things were not only good for the soul.

'Well, I'll stop going on,' she said, breaking into his thoughts. 'I promised my gorgeous granddaughter I'd catch up on Peppa Pig. Billy's in the kitchen, you know the way. Don't be a stranger now, Denis.'

And with that, she sloped off and into the room on the left, closing the door behind her. Hamilton smiled again. The fragrant smell of potpourri filled his nostrils as he walked down the hallway and entered the large kitchen at the rear of the house. Billy sat at the table, which was covered in mountains of paperwork, and held his head in his hands. The shadow of his beard grew down his cheeks and neck, the flickers of grey hair more evident than before.

'Can I sit?' Hamilton asked.

Billy raised his head, but refused to make eye-contact. 'Come to accuse me of murdering anyone else?'

Despite the cold reception, Hamilton took a seat on the other side of the table. 'Come on, you must understand how your actions appeared to me.'

Billy sighed. 'Yeah, and I suppose you weren't totally off the mark. When I heard that Donna's case had been reopened, I worried, always wondering if I actually *was* the last person to see her. But I didn't do it to use you; I wanted your help and support. Something you've always given me, and I'm sorry I didn't repay the favour.'

'What happened? I can't believe you just wandered off to find yourself after Maggie's death … there has to be more to it.'

Billy roughly rubbed his hand back and forth over his cropped hair. 'It all started again, the bullying … and I feel ridiculous even saying that aloud.'

'You shouldn't. It happens, and I need to appreciate that, maybe more than anyone. And not just because my daughter suffered but because of my profession. Billy, every day I investigate people who find new and depraved ways to hurt others, even those they say they love. You shouldn't feel ashamed or silly.'

A slight smile appeared on his old friend's face. 'Despite being a grown man, in a well-paid and respected job, it was as if I was returning to the school playground again every day. It started off small, whispers and funny looks, but escalated to hateful emails and being excluded from social events. Then … Maggie died … and I watched you and hated myself more.'

Hamilton frowned and shook his head. 'What, why?'

'Your whole world had fallen apart, but even in grief, you're a tower of strength. For your wife, your mum; and you returned to work even more fucking hell-bent on catching the scum in this city. What was I doing? Crying in my coffee because the kids at work wouldn't play with me,' Billy said, adopting a childlike voice.

'I wish you'd told me.'

'Ha, and make myself look, and feel, like more of a tosser than I already did? It was a downward spiral for me, and I just had to get away.'

'Does this have anything to do with why you're in therapy? My mum told me.'

'Christ, news really does spread between the old dears. Yes, in a way. About six months ago, Dorinda and I started discussing nurseries and schools for Amelia, and I felt sick. How could I guide my child when I couldn't even stand up for myself? I thought if I had some counselling to fight my own demons, it might help her. But now, without her mother around to help, I'm agonising about the panic returning –'

'Dada! Dada,' a small voice called.

Hamilton turned in the chair to watch a small girl bounce through the room and dive onto her father's lap. Long, brown curls cascaded down her back, and rosy cheeks shone from her pale skin; the image of Maggie's childhood favourite china doll, which had pride of place in the collection she'd kept on her shelves.

'Amelia, I want you to meet my very old friend, Den,' Billy said.

'Hi Den. I'm two.'

He held out his hand, and her little fingers clung to his. 'Hi, Amelia … I'm much older than two, but it's a pleasure to meet you.'

'Pop back into grandma, sweetie. I'll be along any minute now.'

'Okay, Peppa and George are going to the beach. And I want to go to the beach,' Amelia mumbled and left the room.

'She looks like Dorinda, doesn't she?' Billy stated, more than asked.

'Yeah, she bloody does, mate … but she has your eyes.'

His old friend beamed, and something from deep inside stirred in Hamilton. For some reason or another, he'd never had the conversation with his wife, but perhaps there was a chance they could welcome another child into the world. The thought brought with it as much sadness as it did happiness, but it wasn't something he wanted to give up on.

'Look, Billy, I have to head off, but I wanted to say sorry, face to face. I've known you longer than I've known my wife, I shouldn't have jumped to conclusions.'

'Don't sweat it. I guess we're not the same people we used to be.'

Hamilton shrugged. 'I think we are. I've listened to a lot of chat about friendships these past couple of weeks, and I've come to realise how bloody important they are. It's who we choose to have a say in our lives, the people we want to have our backs when we need them the most and who best to have a pint with. Whether we like it or not, they're a mirror of who we are … especially when you've known each other since before puberty.'

'In that case, we'll have to grab a pint together soon,' Billy said and nodded his head, appearing far more masculine than Hamilton felt at that moment.

'I think that could be arranged.' He stood and walked towards the door, stopping briefly to look back at his friend. 'Listen, don't panic about raising Amelia. The fact you so strongly know how it feels to be intimidated and harassed, means you're well equipped to teach her right from wrong. Besides, you're not alone. You have your mum … and me.'

Hamilton left the house of his childhood with a smile on his face and a spring in his step. It'd become clear to him that everyone had their own image of how a friendship should look. From the psychopaths to the ice maidens, and from the jokers to the sensitive souls, everyone craved human interaction in one form or another. He decided it was time to put to bed the demons of his past, the blame and the stubbornness, and embrace the people in his life. After all, Hamilton knew only too well how quickly things could change.

THE END

A NOTE FROM BLOODHOUND BOOKS

Thanks for reading Deadly Friendship. We hope you enjoyed it as much as we did. Please consider leaving a review on Amazon or Goodreads to help others find and enjoy this book too.

We make every effort to ensure that books are carefully edited and proofread, however occasionally mistakes do slip through. If you spot something, please do send details to info@bloodhoundbooks.com and we can amend it.

Bloodhound Books specialise in crime and thriller fiction. We regularly have special offers including free and discounted eBooks. To be the first to hear about these special offers, why not join our mailing list here? We won't send you more than two emails per month and we'll never pass your details on to anybody else.

Readers who enjoyed Deadly Friendship will also enjoy the first two books in the DI Hamilton series, also by Tara Lyons.

In The Shadows

No Safe Home.

ACKNOWLEDGEMENTS

Despite the thought that writing is a lonely job, it's definitely something I've not done alone.

Without my family sacrificing their time, to give me the opportunity and space to scurry away to my writing cave, this book would not be in your hands. There are only so many times I can thank them (so surely one more won't hurt), but thank you for being the rocks I cling to when doubt tries to drown me, for being the shoulders I cry on and the reasons I laugh out loud.

My dear friends (who luckily do not mirror some of the characters in this book), your ongoing faith and belief continue to blow me away. Thank you for encouraging me to reach for my dream.

To the entire team at Bloodhound Books, you are a remarkable bunch of people. I am so grateful to each and every one of you for the unwavering support and confidence you give me. It's inspiring to have you in my corner.

My editor, Emma Mitchell and beta reader, Katherine Everett, have been invaluable throughout the process of this book. Two awesome and honest women, who know their stuff when it comes to crime books, I'm delighted to have worked with you both. To the eagle-eyed Jo Edwards, thank you for taking time out of your busy schedule to help tidy up the lingering errors.

And to you, the readers, for coming back to find out more about Denis Hamilton and his team, I send you my heartfelt thanks. A special shout-out to the amazing bloggers (I won't name you all, for fear of missing anyone out) and social media groups like Crime Book Club, THE Book Club, Crime Fiction Addict and Book Connectors; your sheer love of books makes you all a force to be reckoned with. I'm so pleased you've all been a part of this journey.

Lightning Source UK Ltd.
Milton Keynes UK
UKHW01f2103300718
326498UK00001B/10/P

9 781912 175413